SHATTERED DREAMS

LOVE IN THE ADIRONDACKS
BOOK 2

JEN TALTY

JUPITER PRESS

This book is a work of fiction. Names, characters, places, and incidents are products of the author's imagination or used fictitiously. Any resemblance to actual events or locales or persons living or dead is entirely coincidental.

Copyright © 2021 by Jen Talty All rights reserved.

No part of this work may be used, stored, reproduced or transmitted without written permission from the publisher except for brief quotations for review purposes as permitted by law.
This book is licensed for your personal enjoyment only. This book may not be re-sold or given away to other people. If you would like to share this book with another person, please purchase an additional copy for each recipient. If you're reading this book and did not purchase it, or it was not purchased for your use only, please purchase your own copy.

PRAISE FOR JEN TALTY

"*Deadly Secrets* is the best of romance and suspense in one hot read!" *NYT Bestselling Author Jennifer Probst*

"A charming setting and a steamy couple heat up the pages in a suspenseful story I couldn't put down!" *NY Times and USA today Bestselling Author Donna Grant*

"Jen Talty's books will grab your attention and pull you into a world of relatable characters, strong personalities, humor, and believable storylines. You'll laugh, you'll cry, and you'll rush to get the next book she releases!" Natalie Ann USA Today Bestselling Author

"I positively loved *In Two Weeks*, and highly recommend it. The writing is wonderful, the story is fantastic, and the characters will keep you coming back for more. I can't wait to get my hands on future installments of the NYS Troopers series." *Long and Short Reviews*

"*In Two Weeks* hooks the reader from page one. This is a fast paced story where the development of the romance grabs you emotionally and the suspense keeps you sitting on the edge of your chair. Great characters, great writing, and a believable plot that can be a warning to all of us." *Desiree Holt, USA Today Bestseller*

"*Dark Water* delivers an engaging portrait of wounded hearts as the memorable characters take you on a healing journey of love. A mysterious death brings danger and intrigue into the drama, while sultry passions brew into a believable plot that melts the reader's heart. Jen Talty pens an entertaining romance that grips the heart as the colorful and dangerous story unfolds into a chilling ending." *Night Owl Reviews*

"This is not the typical love story, nor is it the typical mystery. The characters are well rounded and interesting." *You Gotta Read Reviews*

"Murder in Paradise Bay is a fast-paced romantic thriller with plenty of twists and turns to keep you guessing until the end. You won't want to miss this one..." *USA Today bestselling author Janice Maynard*

BOOK DESCRIPTION

Her world as she knew it stopped. And then he walked in.

Tiki Johnson had a perfect life. A wonderful career and a loving boyfriend. Or so she thought. In an instant, everything changed. Her boyfriend left her for another woman—her boss—who decided her services were no longer needed. Feeling as though she needs a break from life, she takes the family boat to the narrows for a camping trip. Alone. All she wants is a little time and space to re-group and plan her next steps. She never expected to meet a sexy stranger who offers her a distraction from her problems.

Lake Grant has been going to Lake George for years. He loves to camp and fish and spend time forgetting whom his mother is while pretending he doesn't come from New York royalty. When he first meets Tiki, he's totally amused by her inability to camp, but even more, so that she has no idea who he is. It's a novelty he's not used to. And frankly, he doesn't trust. However, the longer he spends time with Tiki, the more his heart begs him to do the one thing he swore to his mother he'd never do.

Fall in love.

To all my friends from Camp Chingachgook, especially Deb Katz, Clay Mowery, and Andy Potts. You made getting kicked out of the senior unit worth it!

A NOTE FROM JEN TALTY

First, let me start with thank you for taking the time to download or purchase a print copy of *Shattered Dreams*. Without you readers, I would not exist. If you have not read An Inconvenient Flame, the first book in this series, I highly suggest that you do.

If you'd like to learn more about Jared and the rest of his New York State Trooper gang, please pick up *In Two Weeks*. It is FREE on all platforms.

Love in the Adirondacks is set in my childhood happy place. I grew up in Lake George, and many of the places I take you or discuss in this book are near and dear to my heart. The island where Tiki and Lake meet is one that my family and I used to go camping on when I was a little girl. The summer camp that I went to as a child, we used to take three-day hikes to the Narrows. I can close my eyes and transport myself to this magical place and I hope I've done the same for you.

Now, kick back, relax, and let the romance roll in!

1

Tiki Johnson stepped from her office building and blinked out a tear. It rolled down her cheek, tickling her skin like a feather. It glided to her chin and dropped off her face. She lowered her gaze and watched it fall to the sidewalk as if it were a raindrop.

She tilted her head and stared at the place she'd worked at for the last five years. This had been her life. It had been what she thought had made her happy, and in an instant, a dream had been shattered. Her life altered.

It wasn't her office anymore. She'd been *let go*. Her boss had made it clear she hadn't been fired. As if that made it all better. He told her that he regretted having to make the decision to remove her position, but her services were no longer needed. He was closing up shop altogether in six months. He promised to give her a glowing recommendation. He even handed her a name of a firm in Saratoga.

That was a half hour to forty minutes south of where she lived and in the winter, it would be a nightmare. She loved Lake George and had no intention of leaving.

When she'd asked why she couldn't keep her job until she either found new employment or he closed his doors, he'd replied, "The only one I'm keeping around is my partner."

She strolled down Ottawa Street toward the main drag, gripping her cell phone. She'd texted Josh, her ex-boyfriend, whom for the last two weeks she'd been secretly dating again. The only reason she'd been keeping the fact that she'd taken Josh back from her family and friends was because she didn't want to deal with the judgments from her sisters, or the concerned expressions her parents would give.

That and the fact she wanted some time alone with Josh to renew their relationship. They had been through so much in the last year and they still needed time to heal.

She hadn't told Josh what had happened in her

text, just that she wanted to know if he could meet her for lunch. She'd made sure she hadn't come off too needy. Josh hated that.

But she and Josh had committed to making a go of it, which meant spending time together. Since they weren't telling people they were a couple, they needed to sneak around.

It would take time for her family to understand why she had decided to get back together with Josh.

It had less to do with being sure, which is how she suspected her family would view it, but more to do with being selfish and enjoying having her boyfriend back after all the struggles they'd been through.

Her phone buzzed.

She glanced down and let out a sigh of relief. She needed him at this moment, and he came through.

Josh: *I can meet you in ten minutes at Paddack's Pizza.*

Tiki: *Thanks. I'll order lunch.*

As she walked toward her favorite childhood pizza place, she expected Josh to respond with a specific request, but he didn't. He must be busy with work, and she appreciated that he was willing to take time out of his busy day to take his lunch with her.

That wouldn't have happened a year ago—even a few months ago.

They had come a long way, and she was grateful. She'd be lying if she said the sting of his affair didn't still occasionally flicker in her heart.

But that was in the past.

The distant past.

And their future was bright.

Even if she didn't currently have a job. She cringed. Josh might actually like that idea. He was the old-fashioned sort and believed a man should provide for his wife. His family. To the point that he had it in his head that he had to make more money; therefore, he got to make the decisions.

He was working on changing his mindset.

She rounded the corner and was reminded that it was close to the end of June and summer was in full swing. The street was lined with tourists, and the traffic was bumper to bumper. The Fourth of July was less than two weeks away, and even more people would crowd the streets and waterway. It was always chaos, but Tiki loved the energy. She loved the fireworks. She loved everything about every holiday in Lake George.

Josh didn't value it as much as she did. He wanted to relocate south. Some place more rural. A little more country. She didn't understand why. She wanted to buy a place on the lake, like her parents.

He wanted a place in the middle of nowhere.

He would probably love the idea of moving to Saratoga.

But regardless, she knew they would find a wonderful compromise. She'd worked too hard to mend this relationship not to.

"Welcome to Paddack's," the hostess said. "Feel free to take a seat wherever you'd like."

"Thank you." It was only eleven thirty, so she was lucky that the restaurant wasn't crowded. She snagged the table next to the window. The waitress came by right away and she ordered a large pepperoni and sausage pizza with extra cheese on a thin crust.

It was Josh's favorite and she decided since he was doing her a favor by taking time out of his busy work schedule, it was the right thing to do. Besides, he really hated a Hawaiian pie. There was no point in doing half and half. He always complained that his half tasted like pineapple when she did that and she could do with some comfort food. A crispy crust loaded with meat and tons of cheese sounded like perfection.

She sipped on her water with a wedge of lemon

while she waited. Every time the door opened, she turned. Tears burned her eyes, but she didn't let them come sailing down her cheeks. She reminded herself that she had Josh on her side.

And both her sisters.

Finally.

It felt so good to have Tayla back and living in Lake George. Granted, Tayla was still as busy as ever between opening up her own boutique and creating her very own brand of clothing. Not to mention being engaged. Gael was a wonderful man and he brought out the best in Tayla.

Tiki was truly happy for her sister and Tayla spent more time with the family. Sunday dinners were back and so were the three musketeers.

Life was good.

She'd find another job, only not in Saratoga. She just needed to get over the sting of what had happened.

It took another eight minutes before Josh entered. She knew this because every time someone came in, she checked her watch. She shouldn't have, but she did.

"Hey, Tiki," Josh said as he sat down across from her. No hug. No kiss. No what's wrong or what's going on. "I'm glad you texted. We need to talk."

God, she hated how he could be so unaware of her sometimes. She narrowed her stare. "I have some news."

"So do I." He shifted in his chair, folding his hands on the table. He stared at her intently. "May I go first, please?"

Her heart dropped to the pit of her stomach. It was like a dark cloud moved over her table and a quick bolt of lightning flashed in the sky while she counted, waiting for that deafening clap of thunder. "Okay," she managed. She didn't like the look on his face. The way his forehead crinkled. Or how his gaze landed everywhere but on her.

Something was wrong.

"This isn't easy for me to say and you have to understand when we broke up, you made it clear that you would never take me back. I chased you and jumped through hoops, but you wouldn't give me the time of day. I was shocked when you showed up at my apartment, saying you wanted to give us a second chance."

She opened her mouth to say something, but he held up his hand, shushing her. She hated that.

"I couldn't say no to you. I had been begging you to give us a real shot for a long time. To forgive me for cheating on you and I thought I owed it to you—to us—to try."

"What are you saying?" Her throat tightened. She couldn't take a deep breath. Her chest hurt.

"In these last couple of weeks, I've been miserable."

She gasped. This couldn't be happening.

"I'm sorry, Tiki. I don't love you anymore. This yo-yo ride we've been on did us in." He reached across the table, touching her hand, but she jerked it away. "It's not your fault. It's mine. I'm the one who destroyed us when I cheated. I know that and I'm sorry. But I'm also in love with Jules and it's not fair to you—"

"You're in love with her?" Tiki whispered. Her gut soured. Her heart broke into a million little pieces, like fine crystal crash-landing on the tile floor.

"I tried not to be. I fought it because I wanted to give us a fair chance."

"Oh. That's supposed to make me feel better."

"No," he said. "I'm sorry. I never wanted to hurt you."

"Then you should have told me to take a walk when I came knocking. This is cruel. Even for you."

Just then, the waitress came with *her* pizza. She'd

be damned if she was going to share. She reached across the table and took both plates. "I'd like a double vodka and soda with three olives, please," she said.

"Sure thing." The waitress nodded. "Anything for you, sir?"

"He's not staying."

"Tiki. Are you sure you want to be—"

"I believe you just broke up with me so you don't get to have any say in how I spend my afternoon. Now, if you don't mind, I want to enjoy my pizza pie and cocktail alone." She pointed toward the door.

"I'm not leaving you like this."

"Oh. Yes, you are." She waggled her finger. "Consider us officially over. For good this time. Now leave before I have to take drastic measures." What those measures were, she had no idea, but she wasn't above causing a scene. Not if it meant she got to eat her greasy treat without having to stare at Josh's face.

Or fear putting her fist in the middle of it.

Thank God he stood. "I'm really sorry."

"I hope you and Jules have a wonderful life together." Tiki lifted a slice of pizza and folded it in half. She wanted to mean the words. Being the bigger person was how she was raised. It wasn't like her to be spiteful, so instead of thinking all the horrible thoughts that had begun to invade her brain, she did her best to fill her mind with kindness.

It was nearly impossible, but who was she to begrudge them their happiness?

Slowly, he made his way to the door, constantly glancing over his shoulder.

She waved, hoping that would push him to the street.

The waitress returned with her drink. "Here you go, ma'am."

"Thanks," she said. "When I'm halfway done, please bring me another."

"Sure thing."

Tiki stuffed her mouth full of half a slice and downed a quarter of her drink. It burned, but she didn't care. Her eyes stung, but not a single tear would be shed. Not over him. Not ever again.

Jobless.

Boyfriendless.

She slumped in her chair and sighed.

When she'd made the decision to forgive Josh and move forward for real, she had her reservations. Perhaps that was why she had kept it from her family.

But she never expected this.

All her dreams shattered in an afternoon.

She continued to pick at her food, though more slowly. Growing up, she'd never been the kind of girl who wanted to settle down. Her parents called her a fickle fiddle because she went through boyfriends like some people changed their hair color. She used to tell her mother the idea of being with one man for the rest of her life seemed insanely archaic.

Of course, her parents were more concerned with her lack of career focus. But her parents also never understood where that came from.

Where her sisters both knew exactly what they wanted to do, Tiki fumbled through high school and college without vision. Not because she didn't know what she dreamed about becoming, but because she'd been afraid.

When she'd been little girl, it had been because she lived in fantasyland where she could dabble in everything to see what she liked, but the truth was she was terrified to follow her passion, all because one person told her she didn't have what it took to be a real writer.

Not to mention when she told her father she was considering majoring in English, he thought that meant she wanted to be a teacher. He believed that was a good profession. One that was conducive to raising a family. She hadn't wanted that and told her father as much. He made another suggestion based on her interests. So she went to business school and graduated with a degree in communication. At the time, she was dating a guy who went to law school, so she enrolled in a paralegal program and got herself a job at a law firm.

The boyfriend went by the wayside, but the career stuck where she eventually found the job at the firm she was just canned from.

It wasn't overly exciting, but it didn't bore her to tears. When she met Josh, they discussed the idea that when they had kids, she might consider staying home and that idea appealed to her, but not because she was dying to be a stay-at-home mom, but because she needed a change. She wanted an opportunity to re-examine her passion. To find her dream.

That was Tiki's problem and she knew it.

She'd never done the one thing that made her heart pump a little faster like her sisters had done because she'd let other people tell her that being an author was a pipe dream. When she realized that something she dabbled in for herself was something she wanted to pursue and that she'd given up before she'd given it a chance, she brought it to Josh. She'd been so excited to share with him her business plans and ideas for how to make it work. Unfortunately, that hadn't gone over well. He thought she was completely crazy.

He went as far as to pull up the statistics as to how many people actually made money as writers. Or how difficult it was to be picked up by an agent or reputable publisher. Sure, some people made a killing with indie publishing, but that was just as hard and the majority of the money was made by a select few. The rest barely made enough to support themselves.

That was more depressing than losing her job and her boyfriend in one day.

"Hey, sis," a familiar female voice rang out.

Tiki glanced up, shocked to see Tayla standing where Josh had been sitting just ten minutes ago. "What are you doing here?"

Tayla pulled out a chair. "Before we get into that, I want a drink and a slice." She took Tiki's drink, lifted it, and waved to the waitress, who nodded in acknowledgement.

"Help yourself, but only if you tell me how you knew I was here because when I walked by the shop, I didn't see you."

"Truth?"

"Always," Tiki said.

"Josh texted me and told me." Tayla raised her finger as the waitress set two more vodka drinks on the table. "For the record, he's an asshole and I hope he has bad sex for the rest of his life."

"That's something to raise a glass to." Tiki lifted one and clanked it against her sister's beverage. "I can't believe he told you why I was upset."

"What boggles my mind is that you were even considering taking him back."

"It's over," Tiki said. "For good, but that's not even the worst part." She scraped off some sausage and cheese and plopped it into her mouth. She held Tayla's gaze while she chewed and swallowed. "I'm unemployed."

"Wait, what? You quit?"

Tiki shook her head. "My office is closing, permanently. I was let go, effectively immediately."

"That's a shitty day."

"Thank you for not patronizing me."

"Let me text Gael and tell him he's on taxi driver duty, and then let's call Tonya and have her take the rest of the day off so we can have a good old-fashioned Johnson sister drunk fest." Tayla pulled out her cell and tapped at the screen.

"It's so good to have you back." Tiki let a tear dribble down her cheek before swiping it away with the back of her hand. She wouldn't allow herself to babble like a blundering idiot. It didn't matter that her sisters wouldn't care. That they would hold her hand and hug her with all the love in the world.

It wasn't about remaining strong or some such bullshit.

"Thank you." She sucked in a deep breath and pulled herself together. "I would have stumbled to the storefront after I finished my second drink, looking for a shoulder to cry on."

"I know," Tayla said. "I want to really hate Josh. In a way I do. But he did us a solid by texting."

"You want to know what the total sucky part about all this is?"

"I'm all ears." Tayla leaned forward.

"Since he and I started back up, he wouldn't sleep with me. He said it was because he thought we needed to take things slow, but that felt like a bullshit reason and now I know why."

"Oh, we are making a voodoo doll tonight."

Tiki looked forward to a sleepover with her sisters. The evening would be filled with tears and laughter. They would sit outside their childhood home around a crackling fire, sipping red wine and roasting marshmallows while telling dirty jokes and reminiscing about every bad choice in life they made.

But what she really wanted was to hop on the family boat and drive it up to the Narrows and do the one thing she'd never done before as a child.

Go camping. The real kind.

Growing up, the one thing her father could never do was take his family on a camping trip. All three girls understood why, and their dad and grandpa went out of their way to do their own special Johnson family camping right in their own backyard. They would pack up the boat with everything they needed and drive around the lake for about an hour while their grandfather would set up the yard as if it were one of the islands. Every year was a different theme. One year they even did a crime scene.

It was amazing and it helped ease the guilt their dad carried over his late brother.

When they got older, their father offered to let them go by themselves, but they decided the best way they could honor their late uncle's memory was to camp the way it made it okay for their father.

Only, right now, in this moment, Tiki needed space away from everything and everyone. She needed to be surrounded by water and to be alone with her thoughts.

And she wanted to rekindle her passion.

Writing a book had always been the one thing she wanted, but never did. She thought about it every day, but all the naysayers were louder than her dreams.

If she didn't do it right now, she knew herself and the doubts would fester. And then there was her family. They meant well and they would be full of great advice. But it would be about what jobs she should be going after and how she was better off without Josh.

She understood that. The time she took now was about examining everything she let slip through her fingers while she'd been with Josh. Since she'd made the decision to let someone else call the shots in her life.

It had happened slowly and she hadn't even been aware.

But somehow, she'd lost all sense of self.

And it was time to get it back.

2

Lake Grant leaned back in his massive leather chair that at one time belonged to his great-grandfather and sighed.

"Well, that was dramatic." His assistant, Gretchen Colby, entered his office. She tossed her designer bag on the chair across from his desk and raised her leg, sitting her ass on the side.

Sometimes she could be a bit much to take.

"Are you all ready to head to the Bahamas?" he asked.

"I am," she said. "Are you sure you don't want to come with me?"

He shook his head. "You know the drill."

"I do." She nodded. "But before I head home to finish packing, I want to talk to you about the

Langley submission. I think you're making a mistake by not taking it to the acquisitions meeting."

Occasionally, Gretchen got a bug up her ass about an author. He appreciated her enthusiasm, and he would always be open to her comments.

But not this time.

Elizabeth Langley didn't have what it took to be a great author. Her writing was okay, and the plot had merit. That wasn't the problem.

It had been the execution of the editorial letter that he'd sent two months ago. He'd taken a chance on her as an unagented writer, but only because the idea was solid and again, the writing wasn't horrible. He agreed with Gretchen that with some massaging of the material, it might be worth it. He didn't like that Elizabeth had dropped a couple of names that she didn't really know to get into his slush pile, but whatever.

But the problem was that while he never expected any author to take all his notes, he did expect a new one who had never been published before, especially by his company, to try to wow him with their ability to take direction.

She did not.

If anything, she took the story to places he specifically told her to avoid and added things that he hadn't asked for.

In a nutshell, she didn't make it better.

The story was all over the place and it would take too much handholding to correct it.

This was not an author he wanted to work with.

"She missed the mark," he said. "Send my rejection letter."

"What is it that you take offense to?" Gretchen asked.

Lake folded his arms across his chest. "Everything. But why do you care?"

Gretchen shrugged. "I liked the story. I thought it was different."

"It was. But the changes weren't what I asked for and the author decided to go places that were even weirder than the draft. She's not ready. I was nice in my rejection and told her to keep working on her craft. Leave it at that."

"You're the boss." Gretchen stood. "But I think someone else is going to pick her up."

"Wouldn't be the first time," he said. "Is there anything else? Because I've got edits to finish and you've got a vacation to pack for."

Gretchen smiled. "That was it. I'll see you in a couple of weeks. You know how to reach me." She snagged her bag and turned on her heel, heading out the door.

He went back to the last few pages of the last manuscript he needed to calendar off his desk. He groaned as his fingers hovered over keyboard. Glancing at the digital clock on his desk, his heart raced. He was running out of time.

He needed to finish before he left the city.

Three full weeks of camping in Lake George.

Three full weeks of being reminded of his childhood. Fishing. Swimming. Hiking.

He'd even roast marshmallows over an open campfire like he and his father used to on their men only trip, leaving his mom and little sister Brandi behind. Not that they minded. Brandi was all city. She loved shopping and getting her nails done. His dad used to tease that she was born with her palm first, as if asking for money.

Brandi didn't take too kindly to that, and Lake understood why. She was a hard worker and she and Lake would eventually be partners in Grand Publishing. Though that was a bone of contention with both of them.

Brandi had always been overlooked when it came to the business. She was daddy's little girl. Pampered and spoiled and Lake had to push his dad into hiring her and giving her the same position he'd had right out of the gate.

While Chandler Grant didn't hover over Lake, he did over Brandi. At least at first. But over the years, he'd learned she was just as capable as Lake. However, that didn't change the fact that he favored Lake and demanded that Lake always take point.

Especially when Lake would prefer to take a back seat and do something more creative and Brandi thrived on running the business.

But right now, Lake struggled to focus on anything but getting his ass out of this office and up to the Adirondacks where there would be no dealing with writers begging for an extension on their deadlines. Or arguing with him over his dazzling editorial advice.

He wouldn't have to crush dreams with rejection letters or do Google searches for hidden indie author gems.

No marketing meetings or cover design with people who hadn't even read the book in question, which inevitably clashed with the writer's concept of what they wanted to represent their work. The author had one vision, which often made sense, but they were always too close to the story. Too close to their passion for the characters and they didn't know what appealed to the single buyer at bookstores.

The marketing team did, but they often missed the mark because they didn't understand the story's big picture. They weren't invested in all the feels, and more often than not, that first draft of the cover flat literally fell short of conveying the proper message.

Of course, the author and the marketing team weren't focused on the real issue and that was what appealed to readers. That was the rub and always Lake's argument with everyone in those meetings. They needed to focus on the readers and half the time that didn't happen.

However, right now, he needed to finish these notes so he could email this manuscript back to the author. Lake prided himself on meeting his own deadlines and he wouldn't be late on this one. Not just because he promised it would be returned by the end of the day, but because he planned on driving straight from the office to a quaint little hotel at the south end of Lake George where he'd spend the night before hopping on a boat and heading to an island in a grouping of islands called the Narrows.

As a boy, he begged his parents to buy a summer

place in Lake George. His dad was all in. He loved the idea as much as Lake had, but his sister and mom, not so much. They loved the city. Thrived in the environment. Lake enjoyed the Big Apple too. He loved the culture, but the older he got, the more he wished he could work remotely. He tried to take more trips, but his sister worried about the future and about how their father saw each of them in it. He understood where Brandi was coming from, and he promised her that he wouldn't go do anything rash until their dad retired.

But he also told her that he wasn't going to stop trying. Writing was his dream. His passion. She understood and supported him, for the most part.

He only had ten pages left to go, but he also had the editorial letter to write and that was the hardest part. Putting his thoughts into a concise letter that would not only make sense to a temperamental author but wouldn't piss them off too much was always something he agonized over. He understood how much time and energy a writer put into their masterpieces. He knew how close they were to their characters and storylines. His job was to enhance the process. To make the writer's vision pop even more. Not to alienate the author or drive a wedge between him and them.

But it didn't always work out that way and this was going to be an especially difficult letter to write. This was not the book the author had pitched. Not even close.

That happened and sometimes it worked out for the best.

However, this time the manuscript needed a major overhaul if he was going to be able to sign off on it and send it into production.

The problem then became this was a bestselling author. Not one who could sell their laundry list, but they did well enough to allow for some idiosyncrasies and certainly a little more creative risk.

But no way in hell could Lake let him stray from what worked. It had to be in the same wheelhouse and this novel—as written—would end the author's career.

A tap at the door startled Lake. He glanced up.

His mother stood in his doorway with her chin lowered, her brows raised and her arms crossed over her chest.

"Oh. Hello, Mom." He did his best not to sigh or roll his eyes, which was a leftover reaction from childhood.

He loved his mother. He really did. She was the best. Kind, sweet, and full of warm fuzzies. But she often grated on his every nerve. She had a singular motivation when it came to Lake.

To find him a wife so she could become a grandmother.

That had been her life goal for as long as he could remember. Even when he was a teenager, his mom constantly sized up his girlfriends and whether or not they would make for good wives.

It got so bad he stopped dating. Or at least stopped bringing ladies home to meet his mother.

"What brings you by?" he asked. "I thought you had a dinner date with Brandi."

"I do, but that's not until later and I'm meeting her at home." His mother set her purse on the desk and made herself comfortable in one of the chairs. She crossed her legs and folded her hands in her lap. "Your father tells me you're going on vacation. Again."

"I am," he said. "But what does again mean?"

"You just went away a couple of months ago. I'm beginning to think you don't like living near us."

He laughed. "Not true and that was months ago. Besides, this is my annual camping trip that I take the same time every year. It's been on the family calendar for a while." A little white lie he managed to tell because while such a calendar existed, he didn't invite his mother to his personal events. Not since he was in college. She got upset when he traveled and not for the same reasons his father or Brandi did.

His father worried about Grant Publishing and the fact that Lake was still hell-bent on being a writer. His sister stressed over how to handle their father.

His mom, on the other hand, was the kind of mother who would set him up on blind dates and would show up at the bar and watch. If she thought he needed pointers, she'd send him texts.

Talk about embarrassing.

When he graduated, he told his father that if she didn't stop meddling, he'd never work for the family business. He showed them job offers from companies in London and he would take one of them if she continued.

Much to his surprise, she left him alone.

Sort of. It was at least bearable. She became more like a normal mom who simply wanted her son to give her a grandchild.

Another thing that was probably never going to happen. He wanted to achieve something with his life before he settled down and that meant writing and publishing a book. But that wasn't the only reason he wanted to remain single.

The hardest part about Phoebe Grant's son was that at one time she was Phoebe Fontane—the actress who won an Oscar when she'd been only seventeen. And she was the daughter of Ross and Monica Fontane. Monica had also been a famous actress in her day, and Ross a world-famous artist. Some of his paintings were now worth over a million dollars apiece.

Mix that with his father's side who owned Grant Publishing, one of the oldest boutique publishing houses to still be standing, made Lake one of the most eligible bachelors in all of Manhattan.

It was a cross he did not want to bear. Well, being a bachelor was fine. He liked that part. However, every single time he was spotted with any female, the speculations began and that's when his mother started. Three weeks ago, an old college friend happened to be in town and they had a drink together.

One drink.

In a bar.

And the world went crazy.

Every entertainment news reel picked up the story and the speculations had begun.

Was Lake Grant off the market?

He used to be able to laugh at it all. But not anymore. He hadn't been on a date in ten months. Anyone who did want to go out with him did so because they wanted something from him, not because they were interested in him.

He desperately needed an attitude adjustment. He needed to re-examine his life and work on a new approach to pushing his dad into letting him write. His sister was just as good of an editor as he was and just as capable of running Grant Publishing. She had come into her own these last couple of years and had a good handle on everything. She even took to putting their father in his place.

However, after the Kacey incident, his father no longer thought it a good idea that either sibling go it alone. They were to run the business together.

Period.

And for the last three years, his father wouldn't change his mind. Wouldn't even discuss it. Although, Lake hadn't brought it up in the last year, giving things a chance to settle down. He also gave Brandi the opportunity to be more vocal, and she took it.

Now he needed to get a manuscript in front of his father. And his sister. But he had to write it first.

He needed to prove to his dad he had as much talent as anyone else. That he could do it and not because his last name was Grant.

He knew his sister would be supportive. She had no desire to be an author and her passion for being the face of Grant Publishing exceeded Lake's. Not that Lake didn't love the legacy to which he was born, he just saw it as a different vehicle than the rest of his family.

He also wanted out of the city more often and writing would give him that chance.

"Nice try." She pursed her lips. "Why must you try to sneak out without even a goodbye?"

"I don't really do that," he said. Though it wasn't entirely false either. If he had his way, he would call his mom when he was an hour outside of the city and they could chat about all sorts of things, including the fact that he would be out of town for the next few weeks. She wouldn't be thrilled that he didn't at least stop by and have dinner one last time, but she'd make him promise to come over as soon as he came home.

And he'd keep that promise because she would hound him relentlessly until he made good on it.

Besides, outside of the conversations about his love life or book publishing, he did enjoy his mother's company. They had a fair amount in common. They both loved Broadway, where his father tolerated it. So, he had always been his mom's date and they would sit and talk for hours about the play, the actors, their interpretations. Not to mention the costumes.

It would bore his poor dad to tears.

However, he would enjoy discussing the writing of the show. That was the one thing they all had in common.

The love of a good story.

Only, his father didn't like to watch it. He only wanted to read it. He loved the black and white of words. He found novels to be the sexiest of the mediums.

Lake tended to agree, but he still loved movies and binge-watching a good show on television. He found that to be a great way to study character, plot, dialogue, and so many other aspects of storytelling.

However, nothing beat a good book.

"It's just that I spend the two weeks before my vacation trying to clear my inbox and meet all my deadlines. I'm exhausted. Not to mention the media attention lately. That was a bit much and this time ignoring it didn't seem to work."

She lifted her hands and waved them dramatically. "I had nothing to do with that."

"I never said you did."

"But you know that I wouldn't mind if you and Sarah did become a thing."

"She has a boyfriend who isn't handling all this too well." Lake felt horrible about all the stories circulating in the tabloids and how pictures of him and Sarah from their college days were resurfacing. They had dated for about six months their senior year; however, it had been his first real public relationship.

When they parted ways, it had been because she took a job in Europe. At first, he honestly thought he'd be lost without her, but what they both found out was that they were better friends than boyfriend and girlfriend and that's how they remained.

"His family had all thought they broke up." Lake had firsthand knowledge of something no else did and that was Paolo planned on proposing soon. He had called Lake for a recommendation on a good jeweler to design a ring for Sarah, and Lake was happy to help.

Over the years, he and Paolo had become good friends—no, best friends—so this kind of drama no one needed.

"It has caused them all a lot of grief."

"We've all had some explaining to do privately." His mom squared her shoulders. "You could make a statement."

His mother had a point, but it wouldn't put the rumors to bed. The damage was done and there would still be people perpetuating the idea that he and Sarah had or were still having an affair.

"No. Eventually it will die down. Someone else will become the story." It just sucked that he and Sarah couldn't be friends the same way other people could. Even his friendship with Paolo could be tainted for some time in the public eye.

"You know that doesn't always work in our family and that's in part why I'm here."

"You mean this isn't just a send-off?"

"Your father thought I should wait until after you returned from your vacation, but I worried you might find out while you were gone since it will be announced a week from today."

Lake swallowed. His mother hadn't made any major declarations in years. Her last feature film had been when he'd been a toddler. She'd been nominated for an Oscar, but hadn't won. After that, she turned her attention to Broadway where she starred in three different shows, all giving her critical acclaim. But it had been a few years and she focused her time now on her volunteer work and charities. Though she did appear in a few television shows and made for TV movies occasionally.

His mother was considered New York royalty.

Someone once said that when Phoebe Grant walked into a room, even if it was in her pajamas without a stitch of makeup, she glittered.

Lake agreed with that statement.

Every so often, someone asked her if she planned on making a comeback to the big screen and his mother always replied with *never say never.*

"I generally completely unplug except for making sure I can keep in contact with you and Dad, but inevitably, news makes it to me, so if this is huge, lay it on me now so I can digest it."

His mom shifted—almost uncomfortably—if that was possible. She cleared her throat, raising her hand in a delicate fist over her mouth. "It appears that there will be a remake of *A Girl Named Lilly.*"

"Appears? Or it's happening?"

"Filming starts in two months," his mom said.

Lilly had been the role that his mom won the Oscar for. It was an iconic role and he was surprised that it had taken this long for someone to decide to remake the movie. "Who did they cast to play Lilly?"

"Jennifer Allen, of course. She's perfect to play the part, but what's interesting is who they begged to play Lilly's mother."

Lake's heart dropped to the pit of his stomach and burned as if it landed in a vat of rubbing alcohol. He pounded his chest. "You've got to be kidding? Are you going to do it?"

"I signed the contract this morning."

He tried to suck in a deep breath, but nothing happened. No oxygen filled his lungs. The hype that this would create would be insane. Between Jennifer, who was coming off her third Oscar, and his mom returning to the film that made her famous, the media frenzy would be like a hurricane clashing with a nuclear bomb.

"I couldn't turn it down," his mom said softly. "I didn't search this out. They came to me and your father and I discussed it at length before I agreed. I know it pulls you right back into the spotlight. I also understand how much you hate that, but—"

He raised his hand. "Mom. This one isn't about me." He stood and made his way to the other side of the mahogany desk. He took his mother by the hands and helped her to her feet. Ever since his mom had turned sixty, she'd felt as though not only was she past her prime, but that she might never be on the big screen again. The opportunities for her to act were becoming few and far between and he knew how much that bothered his mom. Teaching acting classes and being involved wasn't enough. His mom still had a thirst for the spotlight and who was he to deny her a dream. "If this is what you want, then I'm truly happy for you. I really am."

"Oh, Lake. Thank you. I was worried how you might respond." She kissed his cheek. "I will do my best to respect your privacy. I really will. I know how much you hate being interviewed and having your picture taken."

"Just promise me you won't try to fix me up with Jennifer."

His mother frowned. "Why not? She's beautiful and perfectly sweet. I've met her a few times and her family is—"

"Mother. Don't." He dated an actress once and while he liked her, he didn't take to the lifestyle much.

"You're going to meet her regardless because of the movie."

"That's one thing, but don't you dare go stirring up shit. I'm serious. Do I need to remind you of what happened the last time?"

"No. You don't. That was totally embarrassing."

His mom patted the side of his face. "I don't know why you refuse to date. You have to be lonely."

"I'm perfectly happy." With the exception of one thing, but he wasn't about to try to elicit his mother's help. That would give her leverage. Which meant her meddling in his love life. "Now, I'm sorry, but I have work to do before I leave for vacation. I promise I will call you when I'm on my way home and we will have dinner and catch up."

"Thank you for being supportive and all that will go with it."

He inwardly groaned. "I will do my best." He lifted his mother's hand and kissed the back of it. "I will be at premiers and show up where family would be expected."

"That's all I need," his mother said. "But if you talk to your sister before tonight, please don't tell her. I want to be the one to break the news, okay?"

"No worries."

Like the movie star she was, his mother strolled out of his office.

He plopped back down behind his desk and pulled up the manuscript he'd been working on and tried not to focus on the fact that when he returned to Manhattan, the entire city—no, the entire entertainment community—would be buzzing with the news that his mother was going to back doing what she did best.

And he was going to have to suck it up and deal with the flashing lights of the paparazzi.

Wonderful.

Well, at least he'd have three weeks of alone time where hopefully, no one would find him when the big news hit the airwaves.

3

Tiki tossed her duffel bag onto the bow of her parents' boat. A shot of adrenaline hit her bloodstream like a lightning bolt.

"I don't like you going alone," her father said.

"She'll be fine." Her grandpa smiled and gave her a reassuring nod. "Cell phone service is much better in the islands than it used to be; plus, she's not far from Glen Island. Not to mention this is a popular time to camp. There will be plenty of people around. Don't worry."

"I'm shocked you're not panicking," her father said, staring at his dad.

For a brief moment, Tiki contemplated canceling her trip. No one in her family had been on an actual real camping trip since her uncle had died, which had been when her mom had been pregnant with her little sister Tonya.

Her father and his brother Richard used to go camping every summer—just the two of them—since they were young boys. They started by doing single nights on Long Island and eventually entire weeks up in the Narrows or the Mother Bunch. But after Richard died, her dad simply couldn't bring himself to go on any camping trip. Not even when his cousins went. Her dad and grandfather could barely take the boat and drive through the islands that first year because of all the memories that would bombard their brains. The last thing she wanted was to cause them any pain. Her grandfather had begged her to go. Her father understood, though his worry came from a place of simply being a father. At least that's what he told her and she had to believe him.

This trip was about putting her head on straight.

Finding her creative mojo so she could find out if she had what it took without that tiny voice telling her she sucked.

"She's a grown woman. She can take care of herself," her grandpa said.

"We didn't prepare her for camping." Her dad

ran a hand across the top of his head. "Sweetheart. Do you even know how to start a fire?"

Tiki laughed. She leaned in and kissed her father's cheek. "I do. But Gael is bringing over his portable gas grill. I'll be able to cook on that, no problem."

"That doesn't make me feel any better," her father said under his breath. "Our idea of *roughing it* had been sleeping in the backyard and your mother used the kitchen, so we totally cheated. You have no idea what it's like to be out there in the wilderness."

"Daddy. I'm going to be on an island in the Narrows. That's only, what? Maybe fourteen miles away by boat. I can be home in a flash." Her father opened his mouth in protest, but she held up her hand to quiet him. "I will check the weather every night before I go to bed and every morning when I wake up. I promise not to take chances. All I want to do is spend some time alone to think and write."

"But an entire week? Do you really need to camp that long?" her father asked. "What if you get lonely?"

"Then I'll come home." She pointed. "Here comes Gael and Tayla with the grill and his tent and a few other state-of-the-art things. You know he goes all out."

"I'm going to say my goodbye now." Her grandfather pulled her in for a big hug. "I love you, kiddo. I want you to know that I understand why you're taking the alone time and I support you. Just remember that you're a bright star in a sky filled with dull ones. You'll find your path. No matter how shattered you feel right now, it will come to you. I promise you that."

"Thanks, Grandpa." She held him tight for what seemed like forever, but she knew was only maybe a minute. Her world had literally been turned upside down.

Of all the Johnson sisters, she'd been the one who had her life organized. A few short months ago, Tiki had been the stable sister and she didn't ever think things would change.

Losing her career she could have handled if she had the support of her boyfriend to follow a passion.

But he'd crushed that months ago, and then he broke her heart.

Now she had no job.

No boyfriend.

But she did have a dream and she was going to use this time to put some ideas on paper and make a plan. She knew she was going to need to get a job. Writing a novel wasn't going to pay her bills and she had no intention of moving back home. She could afford to rent the carriage house Jared Blake and his wife owned for at least four or five months before she had to dip into her savings, but she didn't want that to happen.

So part of this trip was going to be figuring out what kind of job she wanted. Gael and Tayla had already offered, but she wanted to do something without having to rely on family.

Besides, she knew nothing about design or retail.

And frankly she didn't want to learn.

"Your mom was packing some home-baked cookies and other treats. I'll go get them." Her dad squeezed her shoulder. "I'll be back down shortly."

"More food. That's the last thing I need," she said under her breath. Tiki stood on the end of the dock as the sun peeked out over the mountains. A few fishing boats hummed down the center of the bay as they raced toward their favorite spots. The waves crashed into the breakwall and rolled back out into the otherwise calm lake. A million ideas bounced around in her mind. When she'd been younger, she'd always loved how her brain worked. She'd see a person walking down the street, or a sailboat floating in the water, and a story about them would automatically fill her imagination. As she got older, she stifled those thoughts. Now the floodgates were open and she couldn't wait to put pen to paper.

She tried to tell herself that it didn't matter if she was good enough.

What mattered was that she tried.

"I can't believe you're breaking the pact," Tayla said. "I'm not bitter. Really, I'm not. Okay. Maybe a little."

Tiki laughed. "I need to do something and the idea of going to a hotel or even an AirBnB didn't feel all that appealing."

"I understand. I do. If I wasn't so busy, I'd go with you."

"If you tried, I would have to toss you overboard," Tiki said. "I need to do this by myself. It's not about the camping."

"I wouldn't have let her join you." Gael climbed aboard the family boat and set the grill in the bow with all the other equipment. "Besides having a deadline, we of all people understand the need to work through some shit and rekindle that passion." He rustled around the boat a bit, securing a few things before jumping back to the dock. "The instructions for the grill and the tent are in an envelope that I just put in the glove box where your registration and whatnot are."

"Thanks. I appreciate it," Tiki said. Driving the boat. Docking the boat. Those were things she'd mastered when she'd been a small child. She had no issue doing that. But everything else regarding camping?

Well, that she had no confidence in herself whatsoever. However, whatever happened could be good material for a novel. That thought made her crack a smile.

"If you need anything at all, we're a phone call or a boat ride away." Gael rested his hands on her shoulders. "There is no shame in asking for help and whatever it is, I can be in and out of your way in a flash."

"You're going to be the best brother-in-law ever." She raised up on tiptoe and kissed his cheek. "I'll send you pictures when I get all set up."

"I have complete faith in you." He smiled. "I'll give you and your sister a few moments."

"How the hell did you get so lucky with that one?" Tiki asked with a big sigh as she wrapped her arm around Tayla's waist. There was no way in hell Tiki would have mustered up the courage to go on this trip had her sisters not pushed her into it and sat with her while she made the reservation.

"I have no idea, but I'm not ever giving him back."

"I would hope not." Tiki climbed onto the boat, offering Tayla a hand.

Both sisters sat behind the console. Tiki stared up at the house. Flashes of her childhood hit her brain like a runaway freight train. Her life had been a happy one, filled with one joyous moment after the other. Sure, there had been heartache, but she had her family to help her overcome all her obstacles. Only, she'd chosen to keep one buried deep in her soul. That had been a mistake. One she'd never make again.

Her parents had provided her with a good home. They loved her and her sisters. Of course they had their dysfunctions like every other family, but for the most part, she could honestly say they were close. She relied on her parents for love and support.

And her sisters were her rock. She'd be lost without them.

But this journey into whatever the next chapter of her life was going to look like she had to find on her own. It wasn't because she didn't want her family's help or because she didn't believe they could help her find her path. Or even that she didn't want to share her new dream.

She needed a little space to grieve the loss of her relationship and accept the mistakes she'd made. She wanted time to cry her eyes out in peace while she examined new choices. Tayla and Tonya understood.

She wasn't so sure her parents did, but they at least gave her the freedom she desired.

"I can keep an eye out for job listings," Tayla said.

"I wish I knew what I really wanted." Outside of writing and seeing if she had what it really took to make it as an author, everything else was merely a way to put food on the table.

A way to survive.

"I thought about asking Jared if there was something with the state trooper office I could do. That might be interesting," Tiki said.

"What about private investigating?" Tayla asked. "I'll be seeing Katie Donovan this week. Maybe she and her partner will have something. I can ask if you want."

"Would you mind?"

"Not at all." Tayla squeezed Tiki's hand. "I'll be on the lookout for anything that seems interesting. Or pays decent with hours that aren't horrible, so you can follow your dreams."

"You're the best."

"I know."

Tiki laughed. "Here comes Dad and he's carrying two bags. What the hell do you think he's got in them?"

"All your favorite foods. Every home-baked item you've ever said you loved. I bet there's even some red velvet cupcakes in there meant to make you homesick."

"The latter isn't going to happen."

Tayla sighed. "I wasn't going to tell you and let you find out when you unpacked, but I stuffed in some high-end notebooks and gel pens for you." Tayla rested her head on Tiki's shoulder. "Tonya and I both know that you can do this. You're going to write a great American novel. It will get published. We have faith in you."

Tiki gasped. While she was done keeping this dream from her sisters, she was still surprised by Tayla's declaration and that they had the time to go buy her a gift. "I'm not trying. I'm going to do it. I hope, but it's not the only reason I'm spending a week away alone. I really do need some time and space away from everything. Away from the possibility of running into Josh and his girlfriend. Away from my carriage house and the idea that I should be getting up and going to work. I need a few days to give myself an attitude adjustment."

"I get it. I do," Tayla said. "But don't go pushing this aside. Ever since you were a little girl you've loved books. I remember how excited you'd get over your favorite authors when their next books would come out and how you'd doodle in those journals of yours when you'd finish a book."

"I still get like that," Tiki said. "But just because I love to read doesn't mean I would make for a great writer. I've never had any real training. My degree is in communication and my career is as a paralegal, not creative writing. While I have a basic understanding of narrative structure and all that, I fear that an agent or editor would laugh in my face."

"Unless you try you will never know." Tayla wrapped her arm around Tiki. "If I can make my dreams come true, so can you."

"I don't have a knight in shining armor with a hefty bank account sleeping in my bed." Tiki hadn't meant that to come out with a dose of resentment because she didn't begrudge her sister's happiness. Everyone had fallen head over heels for Gael. He was sweet and genuine and he adored Tayla. He didn't invest in the business solely because of his feelings for Tayla. He did so because it was a solid idea.

And Tayla was talented as hell.

"I might have someone who is backing me financially, but it's going to be up to me and my vision to be successful. If my designs suck, it won't matter how much money Gael puts behind me." Tayla stood. "I'll see you in a little over a week. I love you."

"I love you right back."

Tayla took the bags from her father's hand and placed them in the bow of the boat before hopping off and strolling up the dock and back toward her house that she shared with Gael.

In less than a month they would be married.

It was hard to believe that her career-oriented older sister would be the first one. It wasn't going to be a big wedding—just family and a few friends. The ceremony would be right in the front yard, and Foster would be taking the couple on a ride around the bay in his vintage boat. Tiki needed to get in the right mind for her sister's nuptials. There could be no sadness or resentment.

Only honest happiness and joy.

"At least I know you have enough food." Her dad planted his hands on his hips and sighed. He stood at the edge of the dock with a crinkled forehead. "I want you to know that I'm proud of you."

"Daddy. Do you know how weird that sounds considering I lost my job and was about to go back to a cheating boyfriend?"

Her father climbed into the boat and went about checking to make sure she had all her safety items. He'd done this at least twice already. She should stop him, but it would only take a few more minutes and it would make him feel better. "What happened to you with your employment had nothing to do with you or your work ethic. It was dumb luck and you'll land on your feet. You always do. You're resourceful that way. You always have been. I've never worried about you the same way I worried about your two sisters."

"Are you kidding. They both had goals when they went off to college and knew what they wanted. I changed my mind like I used to change my hair color."

Her dad let out a short chuckle. "Do you remember when you were about seven or eight and you talked your sisters into starting a small lemonade and cookie stand? You were determined to do it all summer long. You made up a schedule and everything."

"Oh. I remember. Tayla lasted until Stevie showed up for the summer, and then she was all about finding ways to get his attention. And Tonya, all she wanted to do was swim and play with her dolls."

"But you stuck it out and if memory serves me correctly, you made a few hundred dollars and bought yourself some gaming thing."

"You told me if I made enough, I could get it."

Her dad leaned against the center console. "That's when I knew you'd always make it in this world. Even though you might change your mind a dozen times with what you wanted to be or even change your career. I saw in you that determination to achieve and you've always done that. Maybe to a fault, like with Josh." He reached out and palmed her cheek. "You've never liked to feel as though you failed at something. I know you're hurting and you have to go through it. I get that. But I need you to understand you didn't fail at this relationship. Josh did."

She curled her fingers around her father's wrist and leaned into his hand. "Intellectually, I do know that. However, it's hard not to feel like maybe if I had done something differently or been more attentive, then—"

"Sweetheart, please don't think that way," her father said. "Be safe out there. Your uncle and I always had such fun camping." He pulled out a piece of paper from his back pocket. "Here is a list of some of the things we'd do and the places we'd go. Enjoy."

"Thanks, Daddy." She leaned in and kissed his cheek. "I love you."

He hopped off the boat and untied the lines while she fired up both engines.

She gripped the throttles and eased them into reverse. The sun was now halfway over the mountains, lighting up the sky, turning it a fiery red-orange. She turned the steering wheel, pushed slowly down on the throttles, increasing speed, and headed north.

A sense of excitement that she'd never experienced before filled her heart.

This was the beginning of a new chapter of her life. A new adventure.

Her past dreams might have been shattered.

But it was time to create new ones.

4

Lake broke off a piece of a powdered treat and stuffed it in his mouth and moaned. "Damn, that's good." He never ate doughnuts.

Ever.

It was rare he put such things into his body. Maybe the occasional cookie or piece of cake. Maybe some pie on Thanksgiving or during the holiday season. But other than that, he avoided sweets. Now that he was thirty-seven, he didn't metabolize food the same way as he did when he'd been a teenager or even in his twenties when he could eat anything and not exercise.

Now, he had to hit the gym at least three times if

not five times a week. He had to watch what he ate and even gave up fast food.

Okay, he had the occasional order of French fries, but generally, only when he traveled.

He raised his coffee mug and sipped.

Now that wasn't so great. He'd gotten spoiled over the years, but it was caffeine and that he needed to survive. Without it, he'd never make it through the day without being miserable and getting a headache. Later, he'd crack open a bottle of wine.

Before five.

And it would feel freaking fantastic.

He wasn't a huge drinker. Barely drank at all when he was at home. Maybe a glass or two of red wine with dinner a few times a week.

Or the occasional whiskey when out with friends. However, because of who he was and who his parents were, he always made sure he stayed in control. There was nothing worse than giving the tabloids what they wanted. He would not bring shame to his family. It was bad enough that they were constantly trying to stir up trouble and printing lies, so why give them fodder.

However, when he came to Lake George and camped on the islands, he was able to let loose a little. He made sure that he wasn't followed. While his authors knew he'd gone on vacation, they believed he went to a posh resort in the Bahamas where the company jet had flown first thing this morning with his assistant, Gretchen. It was elaborate, but he needed the paparazzi to believe he was out of the country so he could sit on Turtle Island and do nothing but write and fish.

No one would expect to see him there.

His cell buzzed.

He glanced at the screen. Wonderful. His sister. He tapped the green circle. "Hey, Brandi. How was dinner with Mother?"

"Can you believe they are remaking *A Girl Named Lilly* and Mom's going to play Lilly's mother?"

"It's pretty amazing," Lake said. "Is Mom still over the moon?"

"Over it? I don't think she'll ever come back," Brandi said. "I haven't seen her this happy in a long time."

"Maybe she'll forget all about the fact we're both single."

Brandi laughed. "You do know that your status matters so much more than mine. I mean, my wedding will cost them a small fortune for starters, but the bigger issue is, any baby I have won't have Grant as a last name."

"You could give your child that name if you wanted."

"I need to find a husband first and I'm almost as particular as you are."

"No," Lake said. "I'm not particular. I'm just never getting married or having children."

"Never say never." His sister loved that phrase.

He, on the other hand, hated it.

"Listen, I need to talk to you about Gretchen," his sister started. "I heard a rumor that she was seen talking with Kacey."

"Rumor or fact?"

"Rumor. But I want to put Tag on it," Brandi said.

"I'll deal with it." He'd heard rumors about Gretchen and Kacey before and nothing ever came of it.

"Okay, but did you know she made a bid for an author you rejected?"

"Which author and what do you mean by that?" he asked.

"Elizabeth Langley."

"I told Gretchen yesterday to send the letter. When did she talk to you about it?"

"This morning. I called her to confirm a few things and she brought it up. I told her that if you wanted this Langley woman, then it would be brought up at the next meeting, but she went into some song and dance that you hadn't liked the revisions and were being closed-minded about it."

"Gretchen shouldn't have brought it up. I don't understand why she did, but we're not going to extend another revise and submit."

"Fair enough," Brandi said.

"Anything else?"

"Yeah. If you're writing a novel, you better make it the best fucking thing Dad has ever read. I'm tired of being in your shadow."

"Yes, ma'am," he said. "Love ya."

"Love ya right back." The line went dead.

He took another bite of his sinful breakfast and swung his leg over the picnic table, adjusting his baseball cap. He fiddled with the pen in his hand and stared at the words on the page.

Or lack thereof.

Writing on his computer would be so much faster; however, he needed to flesh out this scene idea a little better. He'd pull out his laptop this afternoon and put the words on the screen.

Thank goodness for modern technology and the ability to charge his computer with his boat along with having a long battery life.

The sound of an engine approaching caught his

attention. He squinted as a fishing vessel approached the dock. There wasn't a ton of brush or trees between him and the next campsite. There was some, but not enough. That had always been a problem. One year he had rented both campsites and set up two tents, but that ended up drawing more attention to himself, and not in a good way. People thought he was weird—creepy—and since there was only one boat, that also brought stares and whispers.

It was best to take the risk and hope people didn't recognize him.

He did things like wear hats and sunglasses all the time. He also tried to stay away from crowded areas. But he did hike Black Mountain every year. He also liked to go fishing and sometimes he even drove down to the village or to Ticonderoga. However, for the most part, he kept his butt in a chair and his hands filled with paper and pen.

This was his year. He was going to prove to his parents he had what it took to be a successful writer.

He covered his eyes and noticed there was only one person on the boat.

A woman.

And not just any female.

His heart hammered in his chest as he watched her command her vessel with ease.

Shit. He was a real asshole for sitting there and not helping. He jumped to his feet, setting his cap on the table, and raced to the dock. "Here. Let me help," he said as he grabbed the bow of the boat. "Although you docked this baby better than I could have."

"I did do that pretty well if I do say so myself." The sexy woman with the long dark hair tossed him the stern line after he'd secured the bow. Her hazel eyes glittered like precious gems in the morning sunlight.

"Are you all alone?"

"Does that surprise you?" she asked with a narrowed stare.

"Not sure that's the right word." He scratched the back of his head. He feared he insulted the girl and that was the last thing he wanted. He went camping alone, so who was he to judge.

Or be a male chauvinist.

Sometimes he certainly knew how to open his mouth and insert his foot.

"Would you like some help unloading? Looks like you have a ton of stuff."

"My father would tell me not to talk to strangers." She shut down the engines and smiled.

He gripped the posts to keep from falling in the lake. He'd seen his fair share of beautiful women before, but this young lady was a knockout. And not in the typical actress, model, or socialite kind of way that he was used to seeing at all his local hangouts in New York City. She was a natural beauty. No makeup or fancy hairstyle was necessary.

"But I'd love some help."

"Why don't you set everything on the dock, and I'll carry it up to the campsite."

"Sounds like a plan." She stuck her hand out. "I'm Tiki."

"That's an unusual name. Is it short for something? Or maybe a family name?"

"Nope. My parents just liked it," she said. "And you are?"

"Oh. Sorry. I'm Lake."

"And you're saying my name is different? You're going to have to explain that one."

Shit. His name came from the role his mother had played in and it was well-known in the media that's where his parents had gotten it from. If she didn't know who he was, she would now. "Nothing too interesting. Just a family name turned into a first name." Nothing like a little white lie to start out a friendship that wouldn't go anywhere anyway. He'd soon find out if his cover was blown and whether or not he'd have to move.

Later in the day, he'd drive over to Glen Island and find out when another campsite might open up so he could move.

Just in case.

Being proactive—or in this case paranoid—should be considered a good quality.

The last thing he needed was helicopters and boaters trying to snap his picture.

He took the small gas grill she handed him and hightailed it up to her campsite, setting it down on a flat area next to the natural wood grill. He made sure it didn't wobble before heading back to the dock and snagging the next load.

Based on the way she handled the thirty-four-foot fishing vessel, it surprised him that she had equipment that either still had the tags on it or had barely been used.

"You really don't have to help," she said as she unloaded more stuff.

"If I don't, it will take you all day. Besides, my mother would smack the backside of my head."

"Now you're being dramatic."

"That's a job best suited for my mom."

Tiki laughed. "Isn't that true of all mothers?"

"That's a valid point." He snagged a few more bags. These two particular campsites were up on a hill, which was nice because of the view, but sucked when you had this much crap.

Especially when it wasn't necessary. But he was happy to help. It gave him something tactile to do while his brain worked through his character issues.

Or at least that's what he told himself. The thing was, he knew he was stuck. His plot was solid. He could plot the fuck out of anything. But characters? He struggled with making them vibrant and as real as Tiki. However, he wasn't sure if his issue was because he'd taken the story in the wrong direction or if his character had misled him and the rest of his cast.

Damn heroine. That's what he got for making her so damn complicated. This is what he warned his authors about. Not enough and they read like the two-dimensional piece of paper they were written on. Too much and it gave the reader a migraine and just convoluted the hell out of the story.

Lake checked his watch. It had taken nearly a half hour to empty her boat of all the stuff she'd brought between the bags and coolers full of food. The tent and tarp. The chairs. The two bags of clothes. Not to mention all the firewood and accessories that went with that.

"Are you planning on staying for a month?" he asked as he let out a long breath.

The sun hit her long dark hair, making it shine. Her hazel eyes brightened as she smiled. "I wish. The site is only available for a little less than a week. I'm actually lucky I was even able to get it considering I just booked this yesterday."

"Wow. You sure are. I booked mine a month ago."

"How long are you staying?" She bent over, opened her cooler, and pulled out an iced coffee drink in a can.

"Three weeks." His right eye twitched. He should have lied. There was no reason for him to risk anyone knowing where he was or for how long.

"That's a long time to go without a hot shower."

He laughed. "Nothing like a nice refreshing jump in the lake."

"If you say so." She brought the can to her plump lips.

He caught himself finding half a dozen ways to describe how the sexy brunette drank her beverage while scanning the campsite with one hand on her adorable hip. He blinked. It was time to go back to his own picnic table and let her go about setting up her own campsite. "Well, if you need anything at all, I'm just a few feet away."

"Thanks. I appreciate it." She inched closer to the platform where the tent went and stood there and stared at it as if it would magically rise up from the ground and set itself up.

Part of him wanted to dive right in and help her or better yet, do it for her, but she hadn't asked and she seemed capable enough. Besides, pitching a tent wasn't that difficult. Most could be done with one person. So could a tarp and if she was like most campers, she'd want to do things her own way.

He snagged his pen and paper and made himself comfortable in his folding reclining chair that faced the water, but he shifted it slightly to the south so he could have a better view of Tiki out of the corner of his eye. Something told him she might need his help, but he also had to admit, if only to himself, that he enjoyed her good looks.

She had this natural glow about her, something he wasn't used to seeing in his world. Everyone was always so made up with airbrushed makeup and hair extensions or fancy styles that certainly wouldn't be worn hiking or camping, which were things he really enjoyed doing.

However, most of the women whom he ended up meeting weren't the outdoorsy type. The last girl he dated had indicated that she loved being outside, but her idea of spending time in the wilderness was on a yacht that was fully staffed. Of course, he wasn't really a great outdoorsman either. He wasn't into extreme sports, but he did like strenuous activities like hiking to the top of mountains—if they weren't too difficult. A few years ago, he climbed Mt. Marci in Lake Placid with some buddies from college and while it wasn't overly challenging for him, he wouldn't want to do anything that pushed him any harder.

Even though he'd only known Tiki for less than an hour, which meant he literally knew nothing about the woman, he had the impression that she wasn't afraid of a challenge, enjoyed some physical activity, and wasn't intimidated by a little hard work.

He liked and admired that.

Of course, he was filling in a lot of blanks and he had no idea if he was hitting the mark or not.

It didn't matter. He would do what he always did and keep to himself.

Of course, it was hard since for the last eight minutes all he did was tap his pen against his notebook while he continued to check out the pretty lady who had spread out the tent and currently stood by the side of the platform with her canned coffee in one hand and the directions in the other.

Mentally, he gave himself a good tongue-lashing. If his father were in the vicinity, he would be whispering in his ear about how a woman shouldn't be doing something like that by herself. Sometimes his dad had no clue. A person's gender didn't dictate their ability.

And then there was his mom who would be whispering in his other ear what a great opportunity this could be for him to meet a nice young woman. Of course, his mother would have to go over there first and make sure she was of the right pedigree.

As if Tiki were a dog and that wasn't cool. It annoyed him to no end that his mother could be like that. He knew that she didn't mean to come off that way, but it's exactly how she came across and it left a bad taste in his mouth just thinking about it.

Even Brandi sometimes scoffed about where people lived or what type of job they had. She had high standards for herself when it came to finding a husband. She could pick on their mom all she wanted, but Brandi wanted a wealthy businessman or doctor or some other professional who would have the means to take care of her, even though she could take care of herself.

And not just financially. Brandi was smart and fiercely independent.

He rubbed the back of his neck and went back to the fictional character he'd created and her problems.

He flipped a few pages and went back to the things he'd jotted down last night at the hotel. Everything felt right up until the moment the heroine's best friend walked into the bar and that's when Lake realized that was a mistake. While the heroine would prefer her girlfriend, for the sake of conflict and the story, it would be best if the hero sauntered in.

But why would he go there? What would be the reason? And what happened to Sally, the best friend? Why would she stand up Annette?

Lake dropped his head back and closed his eyes. As an editor he hated clichés, but they did have a place in fiction because sometimes they added a sense of reality that readers could relate to. But they needed to come in small doses and his rule of thumb was no more than three per seventy-five thousand words.

And everything had to happen for a reason. When he asked his authors why, he expected them to know the answer. He didn't always have to have them give him the why, but he needed them to know it.

He had mad respect for his authors. He knew what it took to write a novel and he didn't belittle the process. He did, however, become insanely frustrated when his writers became lazy. But sitting here in this moment, he understood why that happened. It wouldn't change how he handled his authors. He still wouldn't cut them any slack. All it did was make him want to become an even better novelist.

Crash.

Thump.

Thud.

"Shit," Tiki's voice rang out.

He turned his head and tried not to laugh. A soft rumble filled his throat. "Are you okay?"

She managed to stick her head out from under a heap of fabric and metal poles that was her tent that had fallen.

"Oh. Just dandy." She wiped her hair from her eyes and crawled out from under the rubble. "The directions indicate that one person can do this in a matter of twenty minutes. But that's the only verbiage the instructions give. The rest are really bad pictures and the rods don't snap in place like I think they are supposed to."

"Would you like a hand?"

"If you're offering, I'll accept."

He set his paper and pen in his lap and clapped.

"Oh. That's not funny." She jumped to her feet and smoothed down her workout pants that didn't leave much to the imagination. For the end of June, it was unseasonably cold, even for Lake George, with high temperatures only running maybe seventy to seventy-five and the lows in the fifties.

"I'm sorry. That was rude."

"Yeah, well. If the tables were turned, I'd be rolling on the ground laughing my ass off."

"Good to know." He stood and made his way to her site.

The tent was a standard four-man pup tent. It wasn't that difficult at all, but it was new, making the material tight and not always easy to stretch out over the poles. If she'd never set one up before, she might not be able to do it herself.

"Okay. Let's start with opposing poles on the outside. You can take these over there. And I'll do these on this side. It will be tight and you'll need to bend them."

"I know," she said. "I had this, but then when I tried to lift it in the middle, it collapsed on me."

"We'll do that last." He ran his poles through the threads and pulled it tight and then helped her do her side before moving to the other two and finally the inside. It took some strength and one or two adjustments, but between the two of them, in less than fifteen minutes, she had a cozy home.

"Thank you so much," she said.

"Why don't you let me help you set up the rest of your camp? You're going to want to protect your food from raccoons and you still have a tarp and the rest of this stuff to deal with. It will take you until sunset to do it and I'm sure you'd rather relax and do something else."

"Are you sure you don't mind?"

He shook his head. "You'd actually be doing me a favor."

"How so?"

"While this is a vacation for me, I'm actually doing a side project and it's giving me a bit of a headache, so you're giving me a chance to think through some things."

"That's fair, but only if you let me cook you dinner." She waved her hand across all her bags. "My mom sent me with so much food, most of it will go bad."

"You don't have to do that." His heart dropped from the center of his chest to his toes and then lurched right to his throat, beating wildly. His trust level was on high alert again. He didn't want to have to be rude, but he needed to know that she'd respect his need for privacy, if it came to that.

If she didn't already know who he was and had sold him out to the highest bidder.

"I want to," she said. "I insist."

"Listen. I don't want to sound rude, but I came here to spend time alone and—"

She held up her hand. "You don't have to eat with me. Just let me cook for you. Seriously. I have to do something with all these fresh ingredients."

How could he say no to that? "Okay. You have a deal."

"Wonderful. Now would you mind setting up the tarp thing that goes over the picnic table and do whatever needs to be done for the food? I think I can handle everything else."

He glanced around and chuckled. She had so much to unpack it was ridiculous, and he could tell she was slightly overwhelmed and it came out in barking orders. "Sounds like a plan." However, there was so much to like about Tiki. She had a confidence that he hadn't expected for someone who didn't seem to know what she was doing. But he also sensed a vulnerability about her, especially in her voice inflection. While her word choice was strong and powerful, there was a vibration in her throat.

She also didn't hold his gaze when she gave him direction, as if he might reject her suggestion on how to handle her campsite.

The more time he spent with her, the more he became intrigued by what made a woman like her want to go camping alone. Not that he was some misogynistic asshole who didn't think a woman could handle herself, because he knew better. Yet he understood the world in which he lived in, and a lady by herself was more exposed than a man.

He found himself wanting to keep a watchful eye. To keep her safe.

But he needed to protect his privacy. Hopefully, she had no idea who he was, although that was highly unlikely.

Tonight, at dinner, he'd have to find that out and make sure she'd respect his wishes to be left alone.

If not, he'd be sneaking out in the middle of the night and finding a new spot.

It wouldn't be the first time that happened.

His heart pulsed and his throat went dry. He didn't like the idea of not being close to Tiki.

An odd sensation and a wickedly strange thought—one he needed to push out of his mind so he could focus on his novel.

5

Even though Tiki didn't know the first thing about real camping, she did know a thing or two about cooking over an open flame and on a gas grill.

Although there wasn't much cooking that she needed to do thanks to her mother. The homemade stuffed lobster ravioli would only take a few minutes to cook in boiling water. The lemon brown butter sauce had already been made and simply needed to be heated. Though, she needed to be careful not to overcook it.

That would suck.

Nothing worse than burnt sauce on pasta.

Her mother had even put together a tossed salad with fresh honey lemon dressing.

Tiki's favorite.

This wasn't even close to roughing it, but she didn't care. She didn't come to the islands to suffer. She only wanted to be alone with her thoughts. Being hungry or eating crappy food wouldn't give her creative juices. It would only make her more miserable and remind her that she was jobless and boyfriendless.

Okay, those weren't the worst things in the world and she had started to embrace life without Josh. She realized that he wasn't the man for her and that she'd been hiding behind a façade of what she believed her world should look like. It was a false reality. A fantasy. All based on the fear of living her truth.

"What can I do to help?" Lake strolled across the path between his campsite and hers with a wicked smile, a bottle of wine, and two glasses.

Every erogenous zone lit up as if she'd walked into a steam room. Lake made it easy to forget all about what Josh had done and how he'd been too much of a coward to tell her that it was over when she'd asked him if he wanted to take a stab at a second chance.

Early on in her relationship with Josh, Tayla had described him as the safe choice. She also thought he was boring. The worst part had been neither of her sisters believed Josh fit into the family. However, she gave them credit for trying. Josh, however, struggled to find a middle ground with her family. He was uncomfortable with their way of doing things and he couldn't handle any kind of teasing.

That would always be a problem because as kind and as generous as her parents were, they could be as relentless as her sisters. Especially her father.

But Tayla was right. Josh was safe. For the most part, he was reliable. He had a steady job and he had goals. And she thought they wanted the same things, at least where it mattered.

Sadly, that wasn't true.

She gave in to Josh because she didn't want to be wrong. She didn't want to fail at another thing in life.

"You can crack that bad boy open," she said.

"Gladly. It's one of my favorite red wines and since it's a little chilly out tonight, I thought it would be a good choice."

"I can't believe how cold it's been."

"I hope your sleeping bag is a warm one." Lake set the bottle on the picnic table and went about uncorking it and pouring two glasses while she plated the pasta. "The forecast said it could get as low as fifty tonight. But should bounce right back up to seventy by noon tomorrow."

"I'd prefer it to be closer to sixty-five at night and eighty during the day, but I'm not going to complain." She inhaled sharply. Her mother had outdone herself this time.

"My goodness, that smells divine, wrapped in sunshine and a warm breeze right off the New England coast." Lake sat at the table. "You made this." He glanced from the plate that she placed in front of him to her with an arched brow.

"I boiled the water and heated up the sauce." She smiled and pushed out her hip.

He chuckled. "That does take a certain skill."

"For the record, I do know how to make it and do so with my mom or sisters or even on my own, but this batch only my mother can take credit for."

Lake lifted his fork, stabbed a piece of ravioli, and stuffed it in his mouth. His lashes fluttered and he moaned as if he were having a mini orgasm in his mouth. "Oh. My. God. That's good. Like best restaurant in the world good."

"My mother went to culinary school before she married my dad."

"Where does she work?" Lake asked.

"Nowhere." Tiki often wished her mother had

pursued her passion for cooking outside the home. Although, if anyone asked Tessa Johnson, she had a wonderful career taking care of her family. What could be more important than that? Besides, she often sold her cakes and cookies to local shops and she volunteered at the local fire department, cooking their meals occasionally.

She gave to her community, and no one could fault her for that.

"She actually never finished, but she has no regrets," Tiki said. "She still loves to cook and is currently teaching classes at the community center."

"That's cool and this is some seriously good food." Lake raised his glass. "To your mother."

"I can cheers to that." Both of her parents had been super supportive even though they would have preferred she do her soul searching in their front yard. Her mom worried like a typical mother would about Tiki being alone on an island. She wished Tiki had at least taken a girlfriend or one of her sisters with her—the buddy system—like they had always employed when she'd been a kid. Her dad had other concerns, but he'd bit his tongue and gave his daughter the space she needed under the caveat that she checked in once a day and would call if she needed help.

She readily agreed. Not because she believed there was reason for her parents to be so cautious, but because she didn't want them to be biting their nails while she was doing her thing.

"Wow. This is some seriously good wine."' She licked her lips. Gael had expensive taste when it came to wine, and he had expert knowledge. It was the one thing he hadn't been able to give up when he left New York City and his high-powered job, and since Tiki's sister had started dating him, his fine selection had spilled over to Tayla and her sisters.

It sucked because Tiki couldn't afford more than a fifteen-dollar bottle and that was even pushing it, so she didn't drink it all that much.

Unless she was with Gael and Tayla.

"It tastes expensive." She regretted the words as they slipped from her tongue. How rude.

"I suppose that depends on your definition of what is too much money for a bottle of wine," he said with an amused grin. "This one is about seventy dollars at a discount store."

She coughed. "That's insane, even at a discounted price. I'm sorry, I'll never understand why anyone would spend that much on one bottle." She lifted her glass and studied the red liquid before bringing it to her lips, hoping she didn't moan as the full-bodied wine filled her mouth. She swallowed. "Jesus. You and Gael have successfully ruined me."

"Who's Gael and should I be jealous?"

"He's my future brother-in-law and he likes expensive wine too, and now I can't ever go back to the swill I'm used to." She took a long slow sip of the most delightful adult beverage she'd ever had the privilege of putting in her belly. It warmed her throat like the sun coated her skin on a summer day. "Would you mind if I asked you a personal question?"

"I reserve the right not to answer."

That was a fair response. "What do you do for a living?"

"You think that's personal?" Lake arched a brow.

"Well, I'm asking because I want to know how you can afford wine that costs so much, which makes it personal and the kind of question I have no business asking."

"Maybe I just splurged for my vacation." He tilted his head and waved his glass in her direction with a snarky twinkle in his eye.

She narrowed her stare. "Your everyday average vacationer doesn't bring expensive wine camping. They bring beer. Seltzer. Or wine in a can. Whatever they can get at the corner store or Glen Island.

Unless they are celebrating. On their honeymoon. Or something like that. So, why this?" She raised her real glass. Another thing that told her Lake was someone who had more than expensive taste.

He had money in his pocket.

Not that she cared.

She was simply interested.

Intrigued.

Taking note so she could better understand people. This was how she could make good characters for her novel.

She hoped.

This was research for her book. At least that was the lie she told herself.

"Bringing this brand on my camping trip is tradition for me." He wiped his mouth with the napkin and pushed his plate aside. "While I'm on vacation from my day job, I'm still working."

"Now that makes me want to ask two questions." Her mind went into overdrive. It wasn't about writing anymore. She wanted to know what made him tick. Why he was the way he was and what possessed him to do the things he did. She could say it was research all she wanted, but she was only kidding herself.

Lake intrigued her emotionally.

Intellectually.

And most definitely physically. She reached across the table and lifted the bottle. "Mind if I have more? And no, that's not what I wanted to know."

He waved his hand. "Be my guest and ask away."

Right about now, she wished she hadn't had those two vodka drinks while cooking. While they weren't high in alcohol percentage, between those and the wine, she had a good buzz going. No one could ever describe her as being shy, but put a little alcohol in her and she had no inhibitions at all. "I revert back to my original question for starters, and then I want to know what you're working on out here on your vacation that requires the best wine I've ever had." She leaned in, pressing her index finger over her lips. "Don't tell my future brother-in-law I said that. He'd take it personally."

"Your secret is safe with me." Lake winked. "I work in publishing by day and by night I'm working on a novel."

She tilted her head. "Wait. Isn't that kind of the same thing?"

"Nope."

"Okay. What is it you do in publishing, exactly? If you're not an author."

"I'm an editor," he said.

Her heart hammered in her throat. "You've got to be kidding me. Seriously? Are you an acquisitions editor?"

"Actually, I am." He folded his arms. "Why? Do you have a book you want to pitch?" His tone had the kind of bite to it that could only come from someone who felt as though they were on the defensive.

She recoiled. She suspected he got that a lot and it would be rude to sit there and throw herself at him, but Tayla had taken the bull by the horns numerous times when she'd moved to New York City, and it had paid off for her in spades. It was time for Tiki to do the same. Besides, her grandpa always told her that when an opportunity came knocking, you answered the door.

"Truth be told, that's one of the many reasons I decided to go camping alone. To work on a novel. But I can't say I have something worth pitching to an editor yet, so it would be silly for me to waste your time. Besides, that's not why you're here."

"I appreciate that." Lake rested his hands on the table. "To be honest, when I tell people what I do, either they tell me about the great American novel that they haven't written yet but plan to or shove their manuscript in my face and tell me I'm going to want to offer them a contract immediately."

"That sounds unpleasant and I can promise you that I won't do either. However, I do have another question. Do you only take agented material?"

"In general, yes. But that doesn't mean I won't look at an unagented novel. It just depends on how I come across the author. I attend two conferences a year where I take pitches. Those come in from authors who aren't represented. Every once in a blue moon, I find a diamond in the rough. Occasionally, a writer approaches me somewhere and the idea blows me away, so I'm intrigued, and I'll ask to see the first chapter or two. But outside of that, I usually let agents vet the material for me."

Tiki wanted to ask for a business card, but she couldn't bring herself to do it. She could hear Tayla's voice whispering in the back of her mind that she was missing a golden opportunity, but she did have a week before she and Lake parted as neighbors. That should give her enough time to establish the idea she wasn't going to be one of those crazy writers he spoke of.

However, the problem she faced was the fact that even though she had written a few things over the years, nothing was ready to be seen by a publisher.

Or even an agent. If she wrote every single day and her sisters and Gael were still willing to be her beta readers, she might have something in a month.

But that was if all the stars were aligned.

"You don't have to worry about me talking your ear off about my book. I've barely flushed it out and I'm kind of fumbling around with it. So, I'm nowhere near ready to share it with a seasoned editor."

"I don't do this for everyone, but I'll give you my business card, and when your novel is finished, feel free to send it to me. If it's not something I personally am interested in, and if I think it's good, I'll recommend it to another editor at my publishing house."

"That's very kind of you, but you don't even know the genre. What if you don't publish what I write?"

"I know people. If it's good, I'll get it in front of someone who will."

"And if it sucks?" She inhaled slowly and let it out with a swish. That was exactly the kind of attitude that had been crushing her dream for years. Butterflies jumped around in her belly. In high school, most of her teachers told her she had a flair for the written word. That praise continued in college. However, all it took was one person to read some of her fiction work and tell her that she didn't have it. That what she'd written was basically garbage. That no editor or agent would give it breath.

Tiki never took into consideration the source of this critique. Because it came from a person in power and someone she admired, she took it as gospel instead of either one person's opinion or, perhaps, one person's jealousy.

And then there was Josh. His criticism didn't come in the form of a critique of her work. No, he had a special way of making her feel bad about herself in general. He could have been trying to tear her down, something she had to come to terms with, and that was something she didn't enjoy facing.

Her sisters were something entirely different. While they did often give her negative feedback, it was always laced with how much they loved it and how talented they thought she was. They loved her and would always have her back.

"Will you be honest with me? Or will I get some standard rejection letter? Or some kind words like *it's good but not for us.*"

"What would you like?" Lake held her gaze. He had such honest eyes and it drove her crazy. It was as if she could see right past his heart and into his soul. Even with the sensitivity he carried, he also had a touch of mystery to him which drew her in like a piece of candy on Halloween.

"Complete honesty," she said without reservation as she stiffened her spine. "I want to know if I have what it takes."

"What have others told you about your work?"

That was a loaded question. Insecurity settled in her gut, swirling around like a massive hurricane waiting to make landfall. She'd stopped showing anyone her work because she worried she wouldn't be able to take their criticism. If it was praise, she wouldn't believe them, so it was quite the conundrum. "No one whose opinion matters has seen it."

He pursed his lips and tilted his head. "Most authors wouldn't admit to something like that. May I ask how long you've been writing to be published?"

She glanced at her watch. "About five hours."

"Are you writing longhand? Or did you bring a laptop?"

After they'd gotten her campsite settled, she'd taken her computer and sat on the other side of the tent, out of view of Lake, but not so much because she didn't want him to see her, but because of where the sun came through the trees. "I'm doing both, but I prefer the click of my fingers on the keyboard. Plus, my brain works so fast it's hard to write longhand. I tend to jot ideas down and outline. Or at least that's what I think my process will be."

"Do you have a book plotted? Or do you think you're a pantser?"

"Oh, I don't believe in pantsing. That's just one big hot mess of an outline."

Lake arched a brow. "How do you know if you just started writing to be published?"

"I've been dabbling in writing my whole life. And while I don't have anything that I think is publishable, I have written things. Short stories and what I guess you would call novellas since I was in middle school. I've started a dozen novels; however, I never finished one. Not because I didn't think I could, but because it wasn't something anyone thought was a bonified career path. Even me way back when."

"What is it that you do now?"

"I'm between jobs," she admitted. "But I was a paralegal."

"Lawyers are usually excellent writers because they understand the English language better than the average person."

She chuckled. "I'm not a lawyer, but English—specifically literature—was my favorite subject."

"How do you feel about me taking a look at your

work now?" He raised his glass and sipped, but his gaze never left hers and it was unnerving.

Along with the suggestion.

She'd barely shown people she loved what she'd been working on over the last few years.

Sharing it with a complete stranger while it was raw and unedited could be disastrous considering what Lake did for a living. He could take one look at the crappy words she'd put on the screen and her career would be over before it started.

"It's a rough draft. And I mean rough. What I wrote today I haven't had the chance to go back and fix up and make look pretty."

"I've been editing for a long time and there is a huge difference between good writing and good storytelling. The former means nothing if you can't master the latter. I can overlook bad grammar and spelling and even some stupid rookie mistakes if an author has a unique voice and can tell a fabulous story."

"I bet you say that to all the girls."

"Only to the ones whom I help set up tents with." He winked. "This is an opportunity because you happen to be at the campsite next to me and you're not being pushy. I believe I am a good judge of character and you're being genuine with me, so I don't mind. I can tell you if what you're doing has merit and give you some suggestions on where to go so that you have the best chance of getting picked up by a publisher or an agent, or both. Or whatever it is you want. If I were you, I'd take advantage of it."

She lifted her gaze and focused on the setting sun. The sky had turned a breathtaking purplish-blue. A few boats hummed by the island. Laughter filled the cool summer air. "I'll be honest, I'm utterly terrified to show you because if you tell me that I'm so far off the mark, I'll be packing up this tent and going home to look for a real job."

He reached across the table, grabbed her hand, and squeezed. "Writing is a real job and don't let anyone ever tell you otherwise."

"Thank you for that."

"Now go get me your computer and I'll have you email me what you've got."

She blew out a puff of air as if to get rid of her fear. Only it stayed as a big pit of energy in the center of her gut. "All right. But if it's the worst slosh you've ever read, please let me down easy."

LAKE CLOSED HIS LAPTOP. He couldn't believe what he'd just read. He reached for his wine and took a long slow sip, letting the flavor hit every single taste bud before swallowing. It warmed his belly while the alcohol made its way through his bloodstream and to his brain. He'd opened a second bottle after reading the first paragraph.

Not because Tiki's words hurt his eyes and reading her partial was going to be painful, but because for the first time in a long while, he was excited about a writer's words. Actually, excited wasn't the right word. There were moments he had to go back and make notes because he'd forgotten he was supposed to be editing. A writer was supposed to transport a reader into another world. Another dimension.

Tiki had done that and more.

This was exactly the kind of novel his sister was looking for and he wanted to give it to Brandi.

Not because he didn't want to work with Tiki. He'd kill for an author like Tiki. She was fresh and her voice was unique. Strong but with a vulnerability to it. Much like the person. However, Tiki had another quality that Lake admired.

Humility.

And she was honest and genuine.

She was someone he thought he could write with and that got his motor running almost as hot as he was attracted to her and damn, did he want to kiss that adorable mouth.

Co-authoring wasn't something he talked about often or with many people. The last time he'd considered it, the author he worked with turned out to be his worst nightmare, in more ways than one. She didn't want to write with him; she wanted to be his wife. When things weren't going as she *had* planned, she approached his parents and all hell broke loose.

It had turned into a PR nightmare for both him personally and the publishing house. It took a good six months before the press stopped hounding him about the details and what parts were true and what Kacey had fabricated.

The worst part had been the stories Kacey fed the media about how Grant Publishing had been bullying her and ruined any chance she had of being picked up by another house. Kacey had been a midlist author at best. He'd chosen to work with her because she had good ideas and at first, she took his editorial letters and ran with them. He had no idea that she didn't actually believe he was making her work better. That the only reason she took his advice was that she wanted to get closer to him and all her calls with questions about what he really meant and all her praise over his great insight were simple bullshit and manipulation. She wanted one thing and one thing only.

His last name.

Okay, two things.

His name and his money.

Since then, he'd seen a few authors come through his office whom he'd considered, but his parents would have had a fit if he'd ever tried to work with an in-house author again. Of course, they wouldn't be thrilled if he tried it with anyone.

But Tiki was perfect in every way.

Her writing was raw. Emotional. Tenacious. It made him feel things deep in his soul. The characters flew off the page. They were as real to him as Tiki. He could see each person and visualize the setting as if he were there. She'd mastered the art of sensory with words in ways he hadn't seen in years. What she lacked in a plot—which needed help—she made up for in character development.

With his keen sense of plot and eye for content and editing mixed with her ability to write characters and her use of the English language, they'd be the kind of writing duo that was unstoppable.

Brandi would see her talent and she'd understand why he'd want to partner with Tiki.

He and Brandi had discussed at length why he wanted to co-write. It wasn't that he didn't think he had chops. Hell, he knew he did and that wasn't being arrogant. It had more to do with him still wanting to help run Grant Publishing with his sister. That meant his time being split in two directions. Writing solo might be easier in some ways, but that meant he only had to answer to himself. It would be easy to back out of deadlines.

A partner would force him to be accountable, for starters.

But there was more to it than that. It was the thrill of the discussion he craved and he wouldn't get that going solo.

It was the same concept he had with running Grant Publishing with his sister.

He sipped his wine and sighed. Her novel stepped outside the traditional contemporary romance novel. He couldn't label it women's fiction either. It had a suspenseful flair to it as there was a villain, but that's not what carried the story. Granted, if he pulled the bad guy out, the story collapsed, but he didn't care enough about that part of the plot.

That's what bothered him and it was the most

problematic. However, it was fixable. While he enjoyed a great character-driven read, every single one of them needed that superb plot to remind the reader why they were invested so deeply in the people of the story. Otherwise, there was nothing extraordinary and the characters might as well be the reader's neighbors.

That was boring.

Not that Tiki's writing was snooze-worthy. Far from it. Again, not the issue. Now his mind was filled with a million notes on how to fix the plot and not a single word needed to be said about anything else. Not to mention her draft writing was better than some of his clients' final copies that they sent to him with the idea that their novels were perfect.

Not.

His pulse soared and not necessarily in a good way. She had to know who he was. Everyone did. If they didn't recognize his face, they knew his name. He couldn't say *Lake Grant* and not have someone mention his mother, the famous actress.

Or his family's publishing company.

It just depended on which circles they traveled in, and he'd be a fool not to wonder what the hell kind of game that sweet, innocent-looking girl-next-door type was playing.

He closed his eyes and let the full-bodied wine fill his insides like oil coats an engine. The only people who knew his whereabouts were his parents, his sister, and Gretchen. They didn't know his exact location. There was no way his mom could have sent Tiki.

Or his father.

His sister would never.

Gretchen had been a loyal employee and proved it when she tossed her best friend under the bus three years ago.

When he made the reservation, he did it himself.

But that posed a different problem. Anyone could have leaked that information to Tiki or the tabloids for the right compensation. It didn't matter what name he used on the reservation; his face was recognizable, and people talked.

He'd seen writers do some crazy things to be seen by editors and agents. However, with self-publishing being a viable option these days, both with the ease of getting books in front of readers and the ability to make money, this seemed over the top.

So, the questions that remained were, did Tiki really want to be a published author, or did she want something else?

Shit. He hated being so paranoid and this was

the exact reason he would never fall in love or get married.

Ever.

He couldn't trust that any woman he met had pure intentions.

His mother would just have to accept that fact as he had.

However, it was too bad when it came to Tiki because he genuinely liked her as a person and even more so as a writer. So, he was going to have to find out a few things about her before he made any decisions one way or the other.

He glanced toward her campsite. A light illuminated inside her tent. He wondered if she was reading, working, or something else. He'd told her that he'd want the night to digest her chapters and he'd discuss it with her over morning coffee. Knowing his computer and cell phone needed a charge, he made his way to the docks and his boat. But before he did anything, he had a phone call to make. He never liked reaching out to Tag, but sometimes his services were needed.

Lake climbed aboard his boat and made his way into the cabin cuddy. He set his wineglass and the bottle aside before he plugged in his devices, checking the battery life of the vessel. He'd need to start the engines soon to ensure he didn't suck the life out it and have to ask his neighbor for a jump. He tapped Tag's contact information on his phone.

It rang three times.

"Hello, Lake. I saw the pictures of you and Sarah. Is that why you are calling?"

"No. Not unless you have a way to squash that story without making it look like Sarah or I are hiding something."

"Are you?" Tag asked with a slightly sarcastic tone.

"Don't be an asshole." Lake opened his laptop, pulled up a browser, and typed in Tiki Johnson, Lake George, New York.

A few different things popped up.

A couple social media and professional sites. An article she was quoted in for some paralegal magazine.

That was about it. Nothing too exciting or controversial. That was a good thing. But it didn't give him any insight.

"Sorry, man. Just trying to figure out why you, Sarah, or that boyfriend of hers aren't making a statement about it," Tag said. "Tell the world that you're just friends and maybe the rumors will blow over."

"Because just about everyone who does that ends up either guilty or looks guilty."

"So do the people who stay silent," Tag said.

"The latter is the better choice. Besides, Paolo will be proposing soon enough." There was no reason to lie to Tag. He was as solid and loyal as they came. "And before you go telling me that the crazies could spin that as the happy couple trying to hide from an affair, they will leak how he had already been talking to a ring designer whom I recommended. We've got it covered."

"I'm glad to hear it," Tag said. "So what can I do you for today?"

"I need you to look into someone for me. Her name is Tiki Johnson. She says she lives on Cleverdale in Lake George, New York. According to her, she lost her job as a paralegal this past week and she was recently involved with a man by the name of Josh Hannah. That's about all I have."

"Did you do a Google search?"

"I'm doing it now. That's how I learned about her ex-boyfriend, Josh. But there isn't much from a simple search, and from what popped up, everything she says is true."

"How deep do you want me to go?"

Lake rubbed his temples. In all the years he'd

known Tag, he'd only had him do an extensive background check twice. Once on a woman he'd been dating and once on a business associate.

Both times he'd wished his gut had been wrong, but he was glad he'd followed it.

The only problem this time was his gut didn't have much of an opinion. His heart had become hardened over time, and he didn't trust anyone. He knew he had good reason not to; however, Tiki seemed like a nice, normal girl.

Whatever that looked like.

"I want to know if there is any way she could have targeted me and followed me to my current location. And if she did, I want to know why she'd do that."

"That's an interesting request," Tag said. "Where are you?"

"On an island in the Narrows in Lake George on vacation. I booked it a month ago. Using an alias. No one knows. I mean, my parents and sister know I'm in this area, but they don't know the exact location. My assistant also knows I'm in the Adirondacks, but I made it sound like I was staying in a posh cabin. I go to great lengths to keep my vacation spots secret. But that doesn't mean someone didn't sell the intel."

"That's true. But when do you inform your

authors? Your agents? Your staff that you are leaving?"

"I go the same time every summer. So, it's common knowledge, but I don't advertise it. Outside of those who work for Grant Publishing, I don't tell anyone. I don't put that in my email. My assistant deals with everything and if I'm needed, she knows how to reach me."

"Would she sell you out? If she happened to know your exact location?"

"I doubt it," Lake said. "The only people who have seen my face are those who assign the campsites. That's really the only place where I can honestly think there could be a breakdown."

"Okay. I can focus my attention there and if she has any connections to it."

"I feel like shit contacting you about this," Lake admitted. "My mind and my heart tell me I'm doing the right thing, but my soul and gut are in conflict. I just don't see her as being the type. There is something uniquely genuine about her, but ever since Kacey, I don't trust myself when it comes to women in the business who could potentially want something from me."

"I've always known you to be paranoid and pragmatic."

Lake laughed. "Do those two attributes even go together in a positive way." He didn't mean that as a question. Nor did he want Tag to answer. He completely understood the sentiment. "Can you do this for me by tomorrow night? Or earlier?"

"I'm already on it, but if I find something suspicious, you might want more time."

"No. If there is anything remotely out of whack, then I will have all the answers I need," Lake said. "Thanks for your help. You know where to send the bill."

"I sure do. But since I have you on the horn, you should know that your sister contacted me and asked me to look into a rumor about your assistant, Gretchen, and her continued potential friendship with Kacey."

"Have you?"

"I have and I'm not completely sold on it being a rumor, but I'm not sure that it was anything other than a chance meeting."

Lake closed his eyes. "I'm sure it's nothing, but keep on it and get back to me."

"Sure thing. Talk to you later."

Lake made his way up to the captain's chair with a full glass of wine and started his engines. It would take about fifteen minutes to fully charge his cell along with the extended battery pack. His computer was another story. Maybe a half hour. He lifted his feet, setting them on the passenger chair, and glanced toward the stars.

The boat rocked left and right as a couple of waves crashed into the fiberglass. He loved the way it soothed his nerves. Generally speaking, his distrust of people made him feel comfortable.

Not this time. It made him want to jump right out of his skin.

He liked Tiki. He found himself attracted to her in ways that he hadn't been in years. Most women tickled his fancy.

In bed.

Not emotionally.

Those two things he always separated. He never allowed his entanglements to mean anything. If that made him a womanizer, then so be it. He couldn't afford to care enough to want to be in a relationship. He would never allow himself to fall in love.

That would be dangerous.

He tried to tell himself where Tiki was concerned it was her provocative writing that got to him; however, he knew that was a lie. She had this sweetness to her that couldn't be faked. He'd been around enough actresses in his day to understand the difference. Sure, a great performer could portray that on camera.

However, they needed a little help with the proper angles, makeup, and the perfect lines. It wasn't just about how well they acted.

It was the entire package.

His mother always told him the hardest job she ever had was on the stage. That was where real performers stepped out of the shadows and into the limelight. It separated those who needed the crutch of cameras and those who could truly act.

His mother was one of the greats. She understood that she had limitations and what roles she could handle and in what medium.

Television was different from movies.

And both of those were vastly different from stage.

None of them could compare to real life. Unfortunately, some actors and actresses blended their worlds together and that made for messy headlines because they stopped differentiating fiction from reality. They were the ones who believed their own hype. They forgot that the only difference between them and those who went to watch their movies was the fact they got paid to be on the screen.

And that the privilege for that role lost them

some personal freedoms, like privacy.

The double-edged sword of fame.

His mother understood it. Respected it. And did her best to shield her children from it. She didn't plaster their faces on magazines. Or bring them to interviews or push either of them to follow in her footsteps.

The only place his mother chose to disrespect both him and his little sister was when it came to their love lives.

Disrespect was probably too strong a word. However, his mom really wanted to be a grandmother.

Brandi would love to give her one or two, but that wouldn't carry on the Grant name, and he wasn't going to ever have kids.

Not because he didn't like children. He did. But because he would never take a wife. He couldn't get past the initial distrust phase of dating to fall in love.

He polished off his wine and turned off the engines. All he needed to do now was shut off his brain. He'd talk with Tiki in the morning and then make notes before sending back her manuscript.

Then he'd take off on his boat and get some distance while he tried to write his own novel.

The whole reason for his trip.

6

Tiki stepped from her tent and stretched. She wished she could say she slept well, but she tossed and turned all night. The air mattress wasn't uncomfortable, but it wasn't her bed. Not to mention that she couldn't get her sexy editor neighbor out of her mind.

Every time she closed her eyes it was like it was an invitation for him to visit her mind. His short dark hair and scruffy face filled her subconscious and entered her dreams like an invasion of sorts.

She ran her fingers through her hair before finding her shower caddy. Snagging her towel, which she wrapped around her shoulders, she made her way to the dock. The morning air was a bit warmer than yesterday, but still not the temperatures she would have liked. Sixty-five degrees wasn't end-of-June weather, and she suspected the lake wasn't going to be warm either. However, she wasn't about to face Lake without taking a quick bath in the cool waters.

She wasn't a vain woman. Far from it. But she did have standards and she at least wanted to have clean hair and a fresh face.

Shedding her sweatpants and sweatshirt, she adjusted her bathing suit and decided it wasn't worth testing the waters. She braced herself for impact and dove into the chilly lake.

Damn. The shock to her system was instant and mind-numbing. It was worse than brain freeze.

She popped up to the surface and gasped for air. She swam to the end of the dock and quickly found her biodegradable shampoo and body wash. This would be the quickest bath known to mankind. At least the weather forecast called for blue skies and a high of seventy-three. That should warm her up.

Along with a nice tall cup of coffee.

Dunking under the water one last time to ensure all the soap was gone from her hair, she hoisted herself up on the dock and gasped.

There stood tall, dark, and handsome holding her towel and wearing a sexy smile.

"You scared me," she said.

He wrapped the warm terrycloth around her shivering body. "I didn't mean to," he said with a wink. "How's the water?"

"Freezing."

He laughed. "I think I'll wait for the sun to come out before I take my bath."

"That's probably smart," she mumbled as she dried her hair.

"Are you ready to discuss your chapters?"

Her heart lurched to her throat and thumped, making it hard to swallow, much less answer his question.

"I don't bite," he said, arching his brow.

"I need a few minutes to change my clothes and get some coffee."

"I've got an entire pot already brewed." His smile was as wide as the state of Texas. If she wasn't mistaken, he had some good old Southern charm as well.

Although, no accent.

She had no idea where that thought came from, except she was completely overwhelmed.

And out of her comfort zone.

"How about I meet you over at your picnic table in ten?"

"Sounds like a plan." He turned on his heel and strolled up the path.

Letting out a long breath, she stood there for a moment, hoping her nerves would disappear.

But they didn't.

If anything, they got worse.

An editor from a real publishing house was going to give her advice on her novel.

She had considered Googling his name to find out which publisher he worked for, but then she figured that might taint her opinion of him in either direction. Not that she'd spent any time lately looking at publishers and she honestly didn't want to be any more intimidated if he worked for one of the big five. Or six. Or four. Or whatever they were these days. Hard to keep track.

If he did work for one of the big ones, he probably wouldn't be interested in her—a first-time author. But he had to find new talent somewhere. And if he worked for a smaller boutique press, well, she still didn't want to know which one. Right now, all she wanted or needed was feedback.

And he was willing to give it.

She scurried up to her tent and quickly changed into a dry pair of jeans, a T-shirt, and her favorite pullover, though in an hour she'd be peeling that off as the sun warmed the air. Part of her wanted to quickly text Tayla or Tonya for advice on how to handle the sexy stranger, but the other part knew if she did, they would be texting her constantly, or worse, randomly show up.

Time to face the music. She had sent him her chapters and he'd graciously accepted the challenge.

She'd be a fool not to hear what he had to say.

Her heart thumped so hard and so fast she couldn't focus on anything else as she stuffed her hands in her pockets and did her best not to trip on anything. She'd tucked a pad of paper and a pen under her arm. He'd told her not to bring her computer. That he'd made notes and would send them all to her in email, but that she was welcome to take her own notes on paper if she chose.

Lake sat at the picnic table with his laptop opened as if he hadn't a care in the world while he sipped from a tall mug.

"You look nervous." He handed her a cup of steaming coffee that smelled like it came right out of her favorite local shop. It even had a hint of cinnamon.

"I'm utterly terrified." She palmed the mug, stuck her face over the steam, and inhaled sharply. "God, that smells so good. How did you brew it?"

"Are you trying to avoid what I have to say?"

"I might be."

He reached across the table and took her hand. He held her gaze with his wickedly dark eyes that warmed her soul like hot cider on a fall day. He had this sweetness to him that touched her heart. She trusted him and that thought terrified her because she didn't trust easily. Or that quickly.

Josh cheating on her had tainted her views on men and relationships. However, Lake's dreamy stare washed away all her concerns.

That was a problem.

A big one.

She couldn't let him sweet-talk her into anything because she would be defenseless against his brand of charm.

"Right now, I'm just a friend, who happens to be an editor, giving you some solid advice. I have nothing too terrible to say."

That sounded like he didn't like it. She sat up a little taller. Whatever he had to say, she would keep her mind open. She wouldn't get her feathers all twisted. Tayla had been ripped to shreds a dozen times and she kept pushing forward in her career, not allowing negativity to destroy her mojo.

Even when it came from top designers or others

who had control over her destiny, Tayla always managed to turn a negative comment into something positive. Tiki would learn how to do the same thing. Any criticism he had, she'd flip it.

"All right," she said. "Lay it on me."

"First. I want to start out by saying you do have talent. It's raw. It's fresh. And you will be published, I have no doubt."

Goosebumps dotted her entire body. Her lips parted. She blinked. A million words jumbled in her brain, but she couldn't string them together in a coherent thought.

He smiled. "You heard me correctly."

"Wow," she managed. "I didn't expect that right out of the gate."

"I won't lie to you." He lowered his chin and arched his right brow. "You have a lot of work to do if this manuscript is going to be ready to be submitted to an editor or an agent."

"I'm not afraid to make changes."

"You might not like what I have to say."

"I'm ready." She nodded, placing her hand over her stomach as butterflies filled her gut. She picked up her pen and clicked the end, making sure the ink wasn't dry. Inhaling sharply, she let it out in a slow, controlled breath. She honestly had no idea what was wrong with the novel, but she wasn't surprised he had feedback.

"Your problem is with plotting and when I say that, I mean you really don't have one."

She frowned. The butterflies turned to cement blocks and dropped like bricks. "What do you mean? The story is about a woman reconnecting with her past through a house she bought that she had no idea had significance to her family."

"That's another thing. Too much of a coincidence. That part is too random. There's no urgency."

"Sure there is, especially when the hero tries taking it from her—which I haven't written yet, but that's the third turning point."

Lake waggled his finger. "That happens way too late and I fear no matter how well you write characters that leap off the page, the reader doesn't care about what's happening to them. Now, if the hero has a stake in that house from the get-go, the reader is going to want to turn that page from the very start."

Tiki had to admit that made sense. "Okay. But that changes a lot of the story."

"I don't think it does," Lake said. "But the other thing you're lacking is an antagonist. It feels like you're trying to make it the past. Or maybe even the house. But the reader might be more invested if there was someone else who wants that house. For whatever reason. And we can brainstorm ideas if you want, but while I was engaged with the characters, I wasn't with the story."

She blew out a puff of air and thought about what she'd written and where the plot thickened, and he was right. The story didn't take off until the hero came in and told the heroine he had a stake in the house, and it didn't work because she already owned it anyway.

Crap.

She rubbed the back of her neck and tapped the pen on her paper. "So. Good characters but no story is what you're telling me."

"Yes and no," he said. "I'd like you to take today and think about where you might take the story. I don't want you to read my notes or even go into the manuscript, which is why I'm not going to send you my editorial letter just yet. I'm going to email you a step outline and narrative structure worksheet. I'd like you to fill it out and we can meet back here tonight for dinner. I'll cook."

"No. Please let my mother do the honors. I have so much food that's going to go bad. All we have to do is heat it up like last night."

"I won't say no to that," he said. "I'm going to be gone all day. So, I'll meet you back here around six? Sound like a plan?"

"That's perfect."

"I'm going to stop at Glen Island. Do you need anything?" he asked.

"I'm good. But thanks."

He stood. "Seriously. You're a good writer. Trust me when I say that all you need is to focus a little more on story structure. You've got this." He stood and squeezed her shoulder, letting his fingers linger there for a long moment.

Her skin sizzled. Her heart raced while she stared into his intense eyes. Romantic images and thoughts dazzled her mind. In a flash she could see herself taking long walks on her favorite trails. Or sitting at her favorite restaurant in the village on the water, sipping a vodka drink under the stars while the band played country music in the background.

She swallowed.

Hard.

Crushing on him did her no good. As a matter of fact, it pulled her focus and that would only make it harder for her to achieve her goal. She needed to push him from her thoughts.

Josh.

The single name should bring up all the pains of her past. Her heartbreak. Her loneliness. The sadness that had become her life.

But it didn't because the truth of the matter was, she had been over Josh for a while. This moment in time forced her to accept the fact that going back to Josh had been a cop-out. She'd done it because it felt comfortable. Easy.

Her entire life had been set up so she didn't have to take risks all because the one time she'd done that, she'd failed. That wasn't an option. Not anymore.

"In thirty seconds, I've seen you think about a lifetime," he said softly. "What's going on? Did I say something to upset you?" He sat back down, still resting his hand on her shoulder, but now he massaged it gently.

As if he cared deeply for her, which he didn't.

Her eyes burned, but she wouldn't let the tears fall. She'd never told anyone—except her sisters—how much writing had meant to her over the years. It had been her pipe dream. A fantasy.

However, Tayla had turned a childhood dream into a reality. She worked hard. She remained determined, and even though she nearly sold her soul to the devil, Tayla made things happen.

If Tayla could do it, why couldn't Tiki?

All she had to do was step out of the comfortable place she had chosen to live in for her entire life.

"It's not you," she managed to choke out. "I'm terrified of putting my heart and soul into this and it not going anywhere."

"Why? Especially after everything I just told you, which I meant." Lake lowered his chin. "Look. I don't generally give feedback to new authors who submit to me. I can show you a half dozen standard rejection letters that I use where the only thing that changes is the author's name, because *Dear Author* would just be rude. But the reality is I often don't get past the fifth page of a submission. I read every single page you sent me. That says something about what I think about your skills. If I didn't think my publishing house would be interested in you as an author, I'd be saying something like, *you know, you have a strong voice. It's unique, but we just published something similar to that so I can't take it on. If you ever have anything else, feel free to submit.*"

"How many writers have you said that to?" she asked, honestly wanting to know the answer.

"Too many to count."

"How many actually re-submit?"

"Maybe half and of those, I might find one gem. If I'm lucky," Lake said.

"Have you ever told a writer point blank they didn't have what it took to be an author? To make in this business? That they would never be published."

"God, no," Lake said. "That would be cruel and who am I to say that to anyone. I'm but one editor. Truthfully, my opinion doesn't matter. If you don't agree, don't listen. There are so many famous and talented authors—and books—that were rejected numerous times that are now staples in our society. And let's not forget books that have gone viral that to this day critics will say suck. The bottom line is that while I'm the gatekeeper for my publishing house, my opinion isn't always right."

Tiki wished she could believe the words that flew so easily from his mouth. His eyes conveyed a sincerity that only the best actors could fake. It was hard for her to take compliments. Josh rarely gave them out, even when they were in a good place. That had been one of the reasons her family hadn't liked him, and to be honest, it had always been an issue for her as well. She didn't feel supported by Josh the way she should and they constantly fought.

He would tell her that once they got married and

she settled into her role as wife, things would be different.

Better.

But what he didn't understand was that her being a doting wife wasn't a role that fit her personality well.

"So, what you're saying is that just because you think something sucks, doesn't mean it does and you can admit that?"

"Oh. Trust me. I can and I have," he said. "Do you know RJ Montana?"

"I love her writing," she said.

"Well, I passed on her and it's a decision I have regretted ever since. I wish I could have seen past some of the irritating things she does in her novels and helped her correct it. But I had another big fish on the line, which I'm still happy I signed. So, it worked out. But let me tell you, RJ will poke fun at me every time I see her."

"Do you mind if I ask who the other writer is that you edit? You don't have to tell me; I'm just curious."

His hand slowly moved down her biceps and across her forearm. He laced his fingers through hers and squeezed. "I think it would be best if we kept the focus on you. Not who I work with."

Tiki couldn't help but remember when her sister

Tayla had first started out in fashion design and moved to New York City. She'd done everything right and she'd still been burned by a scam artist pretending to be an assistant to a bigwig.

The email that Lake had given her had been a Gmail account.

What editor used that?

Of course, he'd mentioned it was his personal one and that he was on vacation and he didn't want his assistant to see it. Now that she replayed the conversation, she wondered if she were being taken for a ride.

But his advice seemed so solid. So real. It rang so true.

"Okay." She stood. "I have a lot of work to do and you—well, I have no idea what you're doing today, but I'll let you get to it."

It was time to Google Lake Grant.

7

"You didn't have to come all this way to give intel on the girl." Lake secured the bow line that Tag had tossed him, making sure the bumpers between the boats would keep them from damaging either one. He'd dropped anchor off a small island near a YMCA camp at the end of Pilot Knob Road on the west side of the lake.

He remembered once when he was about ten coming up here with his father on a fishing trip. They stayed in a cabin—because his father wasn't overly fond of air mattresses—but they would go exploring on the lake every day. One afternoon, they came to this spot and Lake watched as kids from the camp water-skied in the bay. They also went sailing. He begged his father to let him attend camp.

It never happened. Mostly because his mom didn't want him to and decided that a boys' trip was enough.

To this day, he still wished he had attended sleepover camp.

"I didn't do it just for that reason," Tag said as he tied together the stern. "I'm spying on a cheating husband who took his bimbo twenty-something girlfriend to Saratoga for the weekend. I got the pictures I needed so I thought why not rent a boat and go camping for a night or two. The only sites left were down on Long Island. But I'm cool with that."

"I'd love to have your job."

"Snapping pictures of assholes committing adultery is never fun, but it's something to do between the really juicy gigs." Tag sat behind the center console and handed Lake a file. "So, your girl, Tiki Johnson, is a pretty boring chick. She's got one sister who was a fashion designer in New York City and used to be employed by Anna Declay."

"No shit. Anna's a super sketchy person to work for."

"You can say that again. And Tiki's sister is the one who made Anna look like a fool a few months ago."

Lake leaned forward, resting his elbows on his

knees. "Wait a second. Tiki's sister is Tayla Johnson?" Lake remembered the story well. He'd given props to the young designer who'd stuck her middle finger up at Anna Declay, who deserved to be put in her place. The story only lasted about five minutes on page six before some other celebrity made the headlines, but he remembered because his mother had been ecstatic. Anna had refused to design a special dress for his mom because she was too old and she was concerned about what that would do to her reputation.

His mom had half a mind to find this Tayla woman and ask her to do it just to piss off Anna.

"That's the one," Tag said. "I put a family profile together, which you can read later."

"Thanks. I appreciate it."

"To give you the highlights about Tiki." Tag leaned back in the seat and adjusted his cap. "She was recently laid off from her job as a paralegal. Her boyfriend dumped her for the woman he cheated on her with."

"Ouch. That sucks."

"I would have to agree." Tag nodded. "Outside of getting picked up for a little marijuana in college, she's squeaky-clean. Like boring as fuck. I couldn't find a damn thing that made me want to find out more. Her family has a few skeletons, but nothing horrific. Nothing notable. And she sure as hell didn't come gunning for you."

Lake should be relieved, but for some strange reason, he wasn't. Actually, he felt let down. It was like he got to the climactic scene of a novel and nothing happened.

Or he watched a movie and all the good parts had already been seen in the trailer. Nothing new in the actual film.

He scratched the back of his neck.

"Are you sure?" he asked.

"Positive. I even did some digging into her ex-boyfriend and into her sister's fiancé, who happens to be someone you know."

"Who's that?"

"Gael Waylen."

"No shit." Lake had known Gael for years and now that Tag had said the name, Lake should have put it together when she'd mentioned her brother-in-law who liked expensive wine. Before Gael had quit his high-powered job, he used to take care of the family money. He wouldn't call Gael a close friend, but they had gone out for drinks a few times. Confided in each over a bottle of whiskey a time or two. Gael could be intense and over the top.

When Lake knew him, all he cared about was climbing the Wall Street ladder and making money.

It would be nice to see Gael again. Lake had been saddened to hear about his parents and sister and shocked to find out that Gael sold everything and packed up and moved.

"What I don't know is if she told her family that she's met you," Tag added. "That could possibly change things if someone was looking for a payday, but I really don't see it. They are stand-up people from what I can tell."

"And she's not a reporter or anything." Which would have been his worst nightmare.

"Nope. That she is not."

That certainly gave Lake some peace of mind going forward, but it didn't change the fact that if Tiki paid attention to the world around her, she should know who he was and that right there gave him pause.

"That brings me to Gretchen and Kacey," Tag said. "My sources say they were spotted at a coffeehouse in SoHo. Kacey was there by herself, working on her computer when Gretchen came in. A few brief words were exchanged and Gretchen left. It didn't look cozy, but it didn't look heated either."

"So, it wasn't like they were having a meeting and it could have been totally random."

"That's what it appears to be. I'll do some more digging and if I find out anything else, I'll let you know." Tag nodded. "What's your next move?"

"Right now, I'm going to sit here and fiddle with my own writing." He pointed to his notebook. "Until it's time to go back and deal with Tiki."

"So, I take it you don't want company," Tag said.

"Not really." However, Lake wasn't sure he would be able to concentrate. In the four hours since he left the campsite, he'd written all of two pages. And they weren't good pages. As a matter of fact, they sucked and he knew it because all he could think about was Tiki's novel.

Her characters.

And how to fix her plot.

Worse.

He wanted to race back, pull her into his arms, and kiss her until she buckled at the knees.

"I can take a hint," Tag said.

All Lake had to do now was figure out how to kill a few more hours without going crazy.

Lake helped Tag untie his boat.

"You know how to reach me." Tag waved.

Lake let out a long breath. There was no fucking

way he could sit out in this hunk of fiberglass for hours, staring at his notebook all the while thinking about Tiki.

Nope.

He fired up his engines and pulled up anchor.

If she wasn't at the site, then he'd do his best to work. If she was, he'd talk shop. Or maybe something else.

Shit. He was in big trouble when it came to Tiki.

He gripped the throttles, knowing he should slow down, but instead, he increased the speed.

Getting involved with her would be a huge mistake, especially if he wanted to work with her either by editing or writing.

Three writing couples came to mind.

Shit. Now he was talking himself into things.

The island that he was calling home for the next few weeks appeared. As he slowed the boat, his heart raced.

Tiki sat on the edge of the dock in a bikini.

Perhaps she couldn't concentrate either.

She raised her hand to her forehead, shielding her eyes from the sun before standing as he maneuvered the vessel toward the dock.

"You could have told me you were one of the

heirs to Grant Publishing. Not to mention that your mother is Phoebe Fontane, the famous actress."

"I think the fact that my last name is the same as my father's, grandfather's, and great-grandfather's and that happens to be the name of our publishing company should have clued you in." He hit reverse a little too harshly, but managed not to hit the dock. "Most people know who I am the moment I mention my name, so forgive me if I find it strange that you didn't know me. Do you live under a rock?"

"Kind of," she mumbled as she snagged the bow line and tied it off. "I don't think I could be more embarrassed."

He lowered his sunglasses and cracked a smile.

Her cheeks were bright red.

No one could fake that kind of blushing. Not even his own mother and she was one hell of an actress. One of the few who could cry on cue. As a kid he watched his mother turn on the charm to get what she wanted. The good news was he could always tell when she was acting because her personality changed a little bit.

Except the tears.

That always freaked him out.

"I have a hard time believing you didn't know who I was the second I said my name, especially because you're writing a book. I'm pretty well known in that circle." He cut the engines and leaned back on the captain's chair. This could be an interesting conversation and it could change his opinion of Tiki. It could certainly alter his decision to want to work with her in the future.

"I told you that I hadn't pursued this as a bonified career path. I'm literally just starting out and haven't done my research with agents or editors or where I'd want to submit my work because I have to actually write something that first, I think is good and second, I've gone through more than once."

"That's reasonable." He loved how fired up she was and that totally turned him on, even though it shouldn't. He should feel bad. He cleared his throat.

"What I don't understand is why you're helping me. You work with so many talented people and here I am bothering you with my barely a rough draft that totally sucks." She planted her hands on her hips. "I can't believe you even humored me with all this. Why would you do that? I'm nobody. You're on vacation, working on your own novel. I don't get it."

"Because you're talented." He offered his hand, helping her aboard, and then opened his cooler and took out two waters. Making himself comfortable on the back bench, he made sure there was room for her and thankfully, she joined him.

It was hard not to notice her toned legs and taut stomach. Her intense eyes were hidden behind her sunglasses, but he remembered their exact hazel color. Her dark hair, pulled up in a messy bun on top of her head, caught the sunrays and appeared silky. His fingers itched to run through the strands.

He really needed to control his thoughts.

"I appreciate you saying that, but I honestly don't know if I believe you."

Needing to see her eyes and the truth behind them, he leaned forward and raised her sunglasses to the top of her head. He was taking a huge risk both personally and professionally.

But right now, he saw no other way.

Tag had given him all the information he needed to make the decision. He had intended to come back and play the ruse for a few more days, hoping that Tiki would come clean, only she'd actually been in the dark. He honestly believed her, too.

Time to put his cards on the table.

Shit. He hated being vulnerable. Especially with someone he was attracted to and wanted to work with.

It didn't happen often, but he was going to have to find a way to squelch his emotions.

The work was more important.

However, he'd need to let her choose in what capacity.

"You're going to have to take my word for it." He wanted to tell her to call Gael and ask him what kind of editor he was and how harsh he could be, but that would inform her that he'd done his research about her and that wouldn't help her trust him. Nope. That would make her pack up her shit and go home faster than a speeding bullet.

Maybe his name would come up, and then he can put that nugget in her ear to help plead his case. For now, he'd have to turn up his charm.

"Did you work on those documents I sent you?" he asked.

"I tried, but it was hard since finding out who you really are." She twisted off the cap of the water bottle and raised it to her plump, rosy lips.

Damn. He'd been distracted before by women, but the more time he spent with her, the more he wished his vacation was coming to an end. Not because he didn't want to spend time with her, that wasn't the issue. However, he couldn't focus on anything other than kissing every inch of her perfect skin.

"I'm not some editor-extraordinaire or anything. I meant it when I said my opinion doesn't necessarily matter. I've passed on authors that have—"

"I understand that." She held up her hand. "You are not just any editor. You're Lake Grant. Senior editor at Grant Publishing and you will eventually be the head of that company. If all the publishing articles are correct, that will happen in the next five years."

"My dad has no intention of retiring that soon," Lake admitted. "However, I need to correct you in the sense that my dad—my parents—want both my sister and me to take over as publisher."

Tiki cocked her head. "You don't want to?"

"I didn't say that." He waggled his finger. "But it's complicated."

"What is that supposed to mean? Either you want to follow in your family's footsteps, or you don't."

He set his water bottle in the cupholder and rubbed the back of his neck. The last time he and his father sat down and discussed when Lake and Brandi might take over the reins was the last time Lake brought up his desire to be a published author.

His dad had scoffed at the idea. He tried to tell Lake that it had nothing to do with talent. He actually said Lake could be one of the greatest writers to come out of this decade and Grant Publishing wouldn't print the novel. He reminded him of what his grandfather had done and how hard it would be for him to wear two hats.

Lake went into his argument about how much smarter Brandi was at the business aspect and she could run the day-to-day just as easily as he could.

His dad's second argument had been nepotism.

Lake tried not to laugh considering he had been given the role of acquisitions editor right out of college.

And Brandi the same thing, though that had been because Lake demanded it. Not because his father was going to give it to her. His dad still lived a bit in the dark ages when it came to women in the workplace.

"My sister is better suited to run my family's company, but my father doesn't believe that is in the best interest of Grant Publishing. He's insisting we do it together."

She blinked a few times. "He doesn't want you to write? Has he looked at your work?"

"He has and so have other editors, including my

sister, but he won't listen to any of them." Lake puffed out his chest, his pride and ego busting through the seams of his clothing. Even his father had to admit that Lake wasn't a hack. But his ability to yarn a few words wasn't the problem. Chandler Grant's real issue was the book his father had written.

And published.

And that book nearly destroyed the company.

But that was a long time ago and Lake's father had to deal with the fact his dad fictionalized reality. The worst part was Edwin Grant didn't cover his tracks well and wrote about a scandal that had affected his personal life and came back to bite him, the rest of the family, and Grant Publishing right in the ass.

Well, Lake was smarter than that and he had no desire to write about his life, or anything that had happened in it.

Talk about boring.

Besides, no one cared.

Lake hadn't lived a scandalous life like his grandfather had.

"But my father believes if I were to have a writing career, then I couldn't effectively oversee the day-to-day operations of the company, which he might be correct in, but that's why my sister and I have a plan. However, he won't even look at that." Lake couldn't believe how much he'd told Tiki about his life. No one else had ever been given this much detail.

No one.

He shouldn't trust her, but something about her made him feel comfortable. At ease.

He enjoyed being in her presence as much as he enjoyed the fresh air.

"My sister's fiancé knows a few authors and he's told me that in order to be successful, you have to treat it like a full-time job."

Lake wasn't going to let an opportunity slip by to out his knowledge of Gael. Not if it got him in Tiki's good graces so she'd trust him completely.

"And who is your sister engaged to? Would I know him?" A flutter filled his chest. He didn't like lying, but this was a means to an end.

"He used to live in New York City." She shrugged. "But I wouldn't imagine you would. I mean, it's a big city."

"Humor me."

"Gael Whalen. He used to work—"

"On Wall Street," Lake finished her sentence. "He also used to manage my family's investments. I know him well and he does know a few of my writers." For effect, like his mother had taught him, Lake leaned forward and rested his hand over Tiki's. "You should definitely call Gael and ask him about me and how I work with my authors. He'll tell you how brutally honest I can be and how I don't like to waste my time." Lake contemplated reaching out to Gael and asking him not to tell Tiki about Kacey, but there were stories on the internet and if Tiki did a simple Google search with both names, she'd find an article or two. It might taint her opinion and she might never want to work with him, but it was a risk he was willing to take. He'd have to tell her eventually anyway.

"I might have to do that." She lowered her gaze, staring at their hands.

He should move his, but instead, he intertwined their fingers and rubbed his thumb over her soft sun-kissed skin.

"I'm more curious about the fact you want to be an author and how you can both write and edit. Wouldn't that be a conflict of interest? You'd be competing for marketing dollars and that could be seen as unfair."

"You sound like my dad." Lake had heard it all before and he understood each and every argument. He also didn't disagree with them which is why he would limit himself to certain authors. Ones that were not in his genre. And when he took over as publisher, he wouldn't be able to edit as much. His job would be more making sure his editors were buying the kinds of books that represented Grant Publishing.

He and Brandi had a fifty-page document that showed how he would take a step back, letting Brandi run the company as he took on more of a consulting role, while still editing a handful of clients, and be an author inside the Grant Publishing family.

His father wouldn't hear of it.

Not even with a co-writer.

Especially not after what happened with Kacey. But that wasn't even the point.

All Lake wanted was the chance to prove that he could write a novel that wouldn't bring shame to the family.

Nor controversy to the business.

So far, he'd brought the latter, but he'd do better the next time because he had planned on going solo, but his dad had been even more against that idea than before, stating that editors made for crappy writers.

"I've submitted partials to two of our top editors

using a pen name and I would have been picked up. I think that says something for my writing ability." He pressed his finger over her sweet lips. "Being able to see talent and write are two different things and I know that. I'm lucky I have both. Sorry if that sounds arrogant."

She pushed his hand away. "It does. A little. You will be seen as the man who owns the publishing company and put out his own book using his own resources. And before you go getting into self-publishing, we both know that's not the same."

"Actually, it kind of is because discoverability and getting readers to buy books are just as hard for unknowns and that's what I am. Sure, I can toss money at things because I have it. And I could do that, but that will only take me so far. There are three things that sell books." He tapped her knee. "The first one is controversy. Wrapped in that is the type of controversy because that could be the fifteen minutes of fame kind or the kind that goes viral. It's the latter that truly sells books. The second thing is the most important. And that's if readers are talking about it and they are usually what makes it go viral, and that means you have to have people hate you."

"Excuse me?"

"Think of every book that has made it big. What

sits behind it? A little controversy and readers hating it as much as they love it. If it wasn't the plotline they hated or found distasteful, it was one of the characters that was out of line or offensive. Or maybe they decided the author was a horrible writer or did something scandalous in their past." The blood pumping from his heart to the rest of his body raced through his veins. It was intoxicating. "That sells and we know it. And finally, books that are turned into movies or television shows. However, you need sales for that, so that's more the icing on the cake."

"So, is that what you're looking for when you read a manuscript?"

"No," he admitted. "I want riveting, keep-me-on-the-edge-of-my-seat writing where I forget that I'm supposed to be editing a book. I want the same but different. I want strong, compelling characters and a plot twist I didn't see coming. I don't want a writer who chases trends. Or to write for headlines."

"But you just said—"

"I know what I told you. However, you don't know what readers are going to argue over. Or have an intense feeling about enough to defend or trash and there has to be an entire group that feels this way. A posse, so to speak. I've read books where I wanted to throw them across the room and thought they were the worst thing ever and I couldn't find a single other person who thought the same way. I was an island by myself. And I've read books that I thought were the best thing since sliced bread and again, not one person agreed with me. If the world hates it collectively—well, it dies. Fast. If the world loves it, well, it might do okay. It might make a little money. But that author won't be what everyone is talking about."

"Oh. I see your point." She crisscrossed her legs and rested her elbow on the back part of the bench. "That makes it hard for a writer to know what they should be putting on the page."

"Not really." He stretched out his arm. If he were in a bar, it would definitely be seen as a *move*. A way to get closer so he could touch her, and that's really what he wanted to do. He told himself if he leaned in and tried to kiss her, she'd probably push him away, and then all the sexual tension that had built up in his body would deflate in a matter of seconds.

He chose not to think about what might happen if she didn't reject his advance.

"If a writer is passionate and bleeds onto the page—like you—it will show and readers will be just as passionate. Success comes in different shapes and sizes and I'm not sure I want to be at the controversial level, but hitting the printed list of the *New York Times* is a goal."

"That's a pipe dream for me."

"You'd be surprised at how many people can hit the list. The real accomplishment is whether or not your book has legs and can stay on the list." Lake knew his name alone would catch people's interest. The press would absolutely cover his first novel and they would bring up his grandfather's fictionalized scandals. Reporters looking for a big payday would dig deep into the book, looking for any piece of reality they could glom on to and prove there were more facts than fiction.

Like the juicy pieces of reality that his grandfather had placed in his work.

Something Lake had to make sure didn't happen.

"I need to finish a book first," she said.

"That brings me to a proposal I have for you." He inched closer, dropping his hand to her bare shoulder. A few strands of her hair had fallen from her bun. He twisted them through his fingers.

Mistake. He knew it and he did it anyway. While this was a totally different situation than what happened with Kacey, which was a pack of lies, he didn't need to add the twist that Kacey had accused him of with someone else. "I hadn't planned on bringing this up so quickly. I wanted to see what you did with those worksheets first."

"I did some work with them, but I didn't finish."

He cupped the back of her neck. "That's okay. The mistakes you're making aren't in the areas that can't be taught. You're a natural born writer and this is what you should have been doing all along." His breath caught in his throat. Along with his heart. He should be backing off his advances and focusing on the work. That would be the professional thing to do and what he'd done with Kacey. Of course, he hadn't been attracted to her at all.

"Are you saying that because you want to kiss me?"

The corners of his mouth tipped upward and he nodded his reply. "But I speak the truth."

A slight moan escaped her lips. She raised her hand and splayed her fingers across his chest. "This probably is a horrible idea."

"The worst."

"I just broke up with someone that I'd been involved with for a long time and I'm still upset over it."

"I don't do relationships," he whispered. "Not romantic ones anyway and this could ruin us working together and I really want to write a book with you. I think we'd make a great team."

"You barely know me." She wrapped her arms around his shoulders and scooted so close she might as well be on his lap.

That thought sent him into overdrive. He lifted her up and shifted her body, gripping her hips. "When it comes to the work, I know enough to at least give it a try. If we find we're not a good fit, we go our separate ways."

She took off her sunglasses and set them on the bench. Her gaze tore right into his soul. "What about this?" She pressed her lips against his mouth, gently at first. Teasing him like all the smells of a good Thanksgiving dinner filtering into the living room from the kitchen hours before the big feast.

He dug his fingers into her muscles to keep himself from carrying her into the privacy of his cuddy cabin before making sure that she understood this was a one-time thing.

Or maybe two or three times if it was as good as this damn kiss.

However, his real interest was in the work.

He cupped her chin and took a moment to catch his breath. "This is releasing the sexual tension so we can focus. Nothing more. Nothing less."

"I can get on board with that."

That was the exact answer Lake needed. He stood, hoisting her into his arms and carrying her to the bow of the boat where he gently set her on her feet so he could open the door.

She wasted no time removing her bikini top and tossing it back toward him.

He growled as he made his way into the cabin and crawled onto the small bed. His heart beat in the center of his throat. Tenderly, he took her foot and kissed her ankle.

Immediately, she smiled and bit down on her lower lip.

She'd propped herself up on her elbows and placed her hands just under the swell of her naked breasts.

It had to be the most intoxicating thing he'd ever seen.

Very few women had ever had such a physical and emotional hold on him; however, Tiki wasn't going to be someone he could have sex with and forget. She'd be one of the few who stuck with him for a long time.

He knew that and he also knew he should stop this right now before he ruined everything.

But he couldn't.

His heart had gotten involved and that was something he wasn't used to. Usually, his brain was in control, telling him what to do and how to do it, and his mind was generally emotionless. He lived his life in such a way that he'd never get hurt.

As he kissed his way up Tiki's toned calf and removed the bottom of her bikini, he found himself struggling for oxygen. He'd avoided the kind of woman who he thought was his type for a good decade now.

Strong, independent, self-made.

Those were words that he would use to describe the kind of person he wanted in a partner.

Tiki didn't exactly fit that bill. But she had character. She had drive. Determination.

And she was authentic.

God, that was such a turn-on and not just sexually.

If that made any sense.

Her fingers massaged his scalp and her moans filled the air as he gave each tight nipple attention. He was desperate to satisfy her and worried he wouldn't be able to—a thought that shocked his system.

He'd always been confident in his lovemaking ability. A tinge of guilt filled his mind. In the past, sex had been something he shared with a few discreet ladies who weren't looking for anything. Busy women who were married to their jobs. He never entangled himself with anyone who wanted more than a couple of drinks, a good orgasm, and a see you later.

It worked for him.

And the girls he dated.

Tiki deserved someone who was present in her life. A man who would treat her like she was the most important person in the room. Someone who would give his entire self.

Not crumbs.

She reached inside his shorts.

His breath hitched. He blinked. Twice. Stars filled his vision. He lifted his shirt over his head and tossed it to the side. "Come here," he commanded.

"No," she responded as she lowered his bottoms over his hips and tugged them to his ankles.

He stared at her while she brought him to her lips.

He swallowed. Hard.

She held his gaze and he could barely bring oxygen to his lungs. His muscles shook with intense heat. She was so beautiful. So sweet and kind. He might have only known her for a day, but he liked every single thing he'd found out.

"Seriously. Come here." He tugged gently at her hair. "I need you to stop."

She wiped her lips and smiled.

"You're killing me." He reached between her legs.

Arching her back, she groaned. Her lids fluttered seductively over her lustful eyes while he stroked her insides with the intent of bringing her close.

But not over the edge.

He lowered his head, taking her nipple into his mouth.

Her body rocked first with the waves that gently moved the boat and then with the rhythm of his hand. It was an erotic dance that tortured them both until she begged him to take her.

It took only a few minutes for her climax to take hold of her and spill over to him.

"Tiki," he whispered in her ear, kissing her neck tenderly, his body still quivering from his orgasm.

She wrapped her arms and legs around his body, holding him tight. Her fingernails tickled up and down his back.

Regret eased into his brain. This could totally fuck up any chance he had at a co-author. While his last effort had failed miserably because Kacey was the wrong choice personally, Lake still believed he was more likely to get his parents on board if he had a professional partner than if he went solo.

However, he had developed real feelings for Tiki and that was something he wasn't used to, but he was going to have to file them.

He rolled to his side, found the small blanket, and covered their naked bodies, keeping her close to his side. He stared out the hatch. The sun still shined bright. He thought maybe it might be five in the evening. He would need to find a way to transition from wild, crazy sex to friendly banter to work.

That would need to be a delicate dance.

She kissed his chest. "You're being quiet."

"So are you." He tilted his head and caught her gaze. His heart dropped to his gut like a cement brick. It was as if she could see into his soul.

"This is going to be awkward, especially since we're both still naked," she said. "But I meant it when I agreed that this was simply releasing the pent-up tension that was between us."

He took her chin with his thumb and forefinger. "And is it all gone?" He kissed her good and hard. It was a mistake. He knew it, but he didn't care. "Or do we need to do it again to make sure?"

She patted his chest and pushed to a sitting position. "What I think is that I need to go start dinner and I wouldn't mind some wine, if you still have some."

"I do. And I'm happy to share."

"Good. Then perhaps we can discuss work over dinner." She found her bathing suit and put it on.

He fluffed the pillows and propped himself up. He wasn't quite sure what to say or do. Normally, he was the one reminding the woman he went to bed with of their arrangement.

Not the other way around.

He found this both unnerving and exciting.

"Work? As in you and me writing a book together?" he asked.

"I'd like to hear how you see that moving forward, especially if your company isn't going to—"

"Oh. Grant Publishing has to be the one that picks it up. Trust me. I have a plan. Whether it was for a book I wrote solo or someone I found to work with, though I really prefer the latter over doing a solo project."

She pushed open the door. "Why do you want a co-author more than writing books by yourself?"

"Because I won't be able to write more than one a year. If that. This way, whoever I choose to work with can still have a solo career which will only help the books written together." He held up a finger. "That means I need someone who wants and is willing to do both."

"You don't know if I would even be open to that," she said with a twinkle in her eye. "But that gives us lots to discuss."

"While keeping our hands off each other."

She laughed. "Yeah. We might need one more time. Just to be sure." She kicked her leg up and then disappeared.

He sighed. Tiki was out of his league both in bed…

And in work.

He was going to have to find a way to focus solely on the latter. That's what mattered the most.

8

Tiki pressed the cell phone to her ear and glanced over her shoulder. She should have made this phone call before she went to bed with Lake. But what was done was done and truth be told, she didn't regret it. They were both adults and this was a rebound thing. She'd be able to act as a professional and she suspected Lake would be too.

But she wanted to make sure.

Lake sat at the table at his campsite with a fresh mug of coffee while he stared at the computer screen and her latest notes on an outline that they had hammered out late last night between wild passionate sex and round four this morning.

The song "Save a Horse, Ride a Cowboy" filled her brain.

She hadn't had that much sex since she'd been in college and was surprised by Lake's stamina.

He used the word shocked to describe it. This morning he said he didn't think he'd be able to and that if he could, it would absolutely kill all the sexual tension between them because he'd be utterly exhausted.

Well, they were both completely drained physically.

However, they still stared at each as though they were horny teenagers. Even so, they agreed they needed a break from all the nakedness and decided to focus on the writing. Since eight this morning, all they'd been doing was plotting, writing, and arguing.

Which didn't help the sparks flying. As a matter of fact, all the sparring about what they should write about and how the characters should evolve made her want to dance around the campfire without her clothes on.

"Hey, sis. Is everything okay?" Tayla asked after she picked up on the third ring.

"Yes and no," Tiki said as her sister's voice snapped her back to the present. She'd been gone all of three nights and she knew her family had been worried she might not even make it that long, which annoyed her for a different reason.

"What's wrong? Do you need help with something? Are you lonely? I can come spend a night or two if you want."

"No. That's not why I'm calling, but thanks for thinking I'd suck at being alone," Tiki said with an exasperated sigh. She completely understood why her sister would come at her this way, but it didn't make her feel any better.

"Oh, come on. I didn't mean it like it sounded. Did you ever think that maybe I wanted a night away? Between opening my own boutique, designing a new line of clothing, and planning a wedding, I'm going crazy."

Well, bloody hell. Tiki should have been more sensitive. Her sister did have a lot on her plate. But the last thing Tiki needed was anyone from her family showing up right now. That would be disastrous.

"I'm sorry," Tiki said. "Please don't be mad, but I need to be alone."

"I get it. I do." Tayla sighed.

This was going to be awkward. And bring up a dozen questions. But it couldn't be avoided. "Is Gael close by?"

"He's in the other room. Why?"

"I need to talk to him. You can listen." Tiki added the second part because she knew her sister would be annoyed as hell if she were kept in the dark. Of course, Tiki could have said it was wedding related, but all of that was taken care of and since it was a small, family only wedding with a few close friends, there wasn't anything left to discuss.

"Okay," Tayla said. "Hang on."

Tiki inched closer to the dock, deciding that the further she was from Lake, the better. She made herself comfortable on the bow of her boat, leaning back on the cushions and crossing her ankles. The sun warmed her skin. At least the temperatures were hitting seventy-five during the day.

Of course, she wasn't worried about the nights anymore—that was if she chose to stay with Lake in his tent where she had body heat to keep her all toasty at night.

"I'm back," Tayla said. "Gael is here with me and he's on speaker."

"Hey, Tiki."

"Hi, Gael." Tiki waved to a couple of kids sitting on the bow of a boat as it cruised by. Summer was in full force and normally she loved this time of year, especially now that Tayla was home where she belonged.

"How's the camping going?" Gael asked.

"Interesting," she admitted. "Do you know a man by the name of Lake Grant?"

"I do. Why do you ask?"

"He's my neighbor on the island," Tiki said. "I felt pretty foolish when I had no idea who he was after having a long discussion about books and publishing."

"I'm sure he loved that," Gael said. "He hates it when people gush over him or his family."

"What do you know about his relationship with his parents and his career aspirations?"

"That's a weird question," Gael said. "May I ask why you want to know?"

"He's offered to help me when it comes to my manuscript. When I didn't know who he was, I thought how nice, but I was still super skeptical when he came back with all these gushing compliments."

"Trust me when I say that Lake isn't one to stroke a writer's ego," Gael said. "I have a friend whom he gave editorial notes from a writing contest and it was kind of brutal. Lake wasn't mean. But he's honest.

That's for sure. So, if he's telling you he likes your work, he's being serious."

Tiki actually believed that part. "I want to ask you a few questions, but I need to know they won't ever leave the three of us."

"I can do that," Gael said. "I haven't talked to Lake in months."

"You know that I've always got your back," Tayla said. "Did this guy do something to upset you?"

"No. It's nothing like that." Tiki sat up taller and checked on Lake. He was still at the picnic table with his head behind the computer. He'd told her that her notes and scene draft had sparked an idea and he wanted a couple of hours to run with it.

Then he told her to go ahead and work on her *other* book, which he mentioned was more important at this stage of the process.

Part of her worried about this collaboration.

Was he like an Anna Declay? Could he be using her and would he run off with their idea, leaving her with nothing?

Of course, that was all compounded by the fact that she'd slept with him.

Multiple times.

"I'm breaking his confidence by talking to you, but I need to know if he's ever talked about writing his own books or co-writing with anyone before and if he has, do you know with who?"

"He doesn't talk about it much, but yeah, he and Kacey Bromely talked about co-writing," Gael said. "It was a cluster and it made headlines."

"Kacey Bromely? As in the bestselling romance novelist?" Tiki found Kacey's earlier novels to be riveting, but it had been a good four years since she remembered seeing her name on any list, much less noticed a book being published under that name.

"That's the one," Gael said. "For the record, Lake swore he was never romantically involved with her, but Kacey paints a different story."

"That's important, why?" Tiki tapped the center of her chest. Jealousy had never been a good look. She had no right to be envious of a past relationship that Lake had with any woman.

However, the idea he might have gone around sleeping with potential co-writers made her stomach churn.

"Because she accused him of sexual harassment," Gael said.

Tiki's heart jumped to her throat. She couldn't even imagine describing what happened between Lake and her as anything other than two consenting adults having a good time.

Except, he did hold some power over her and they both knew it, even if neither one expressed it.

He held the cards.

Her talent meant nothing, if she had any.

Damn. She hated doubting herself and she couldn't even blame that on Josh or anyone else in her past anymore. It didn't matter who told her she sucked or how many times she allowed someone to affect her emotions. It was up to her to change how she responded. Only she could do that.

Well, if she'd learned anything from her sister Tayla, it was that Tiki had the power to say no.

"Did he?" Tiki asked.

"Absolutely not," Gael said. "She was a writer scorned, as Lake put it. She didn't get what she wanted from Lake. She was the one who made advances on him. When he rejected her, she went to the press and tried to sell her story. At first, Lake was going to do what he always does when someone spews lies about him or his family to the media—ignore them. However, one of his lesser-known female writers came to him and informed him that Kacey had been secretly asking every author in Lake's arsenal if they had been harassed. Actually, it was more like she was offering them blurbs and promotions in her newsletter and even money to come out against him."

"Shit. That's shady. But how come I've never heard about this?"

"Um. Not to state the obvious," Tayla started. "But didn't you start this conversation off with how you had no idea who Lake was?"

"I don't know editors," Tiki said. "But I know authors. And she was one I used to read. I think I would have heard about a sexual harassment charge."

"There are a couple of interviews out there that Kacey gave that you could find if you dug deep enough," Gael said. "But for the most part, the story got buried. Lake took one press conference denying the harassment, but did acknowledge they were contemplating working together. He left it at that and it eventually died because it wasn't true."

"Did she go to the police with her accusations?" Tiki asked.

"No," Gael said. "She didn't even take it to Human Resources within Grant Publishing. If you go online, in the stories you'll see, she says that she didn't see the point. That Lake would just pay off people to not only kill the story, but to make sure no charges were ever brought. The story became how her story changed and one reporter caught her in the ultimate lie."

Tiki rubbed her temple. "Oh shit. I remember that. Something about she was supposed to be with her publisher and editor on a certain date when she had accused them of something, but it turned out she was at a party with another man and there were pictures to prove it." She had no idea that was Lake. Or Grant Publishing. Hell, she barely remembered the story. But now that Gael had jogged her memory, it was all coming back.

"That exonerated Lake. Everyone wanted him to call her out and ruin her, but he didn't want to do that. She would never publish at Grant Publishing. Most of the major houses blackballed her and her agent fired her. I'm not sure she's done much since then," Gael said. "Trust me when I say, if Lake is giving you compliments about your work, he means it."

"Wait. You showed him your manuscript?" Tayla asked with a shriek. "You haven't even showed it to me yet. I'm insulted."

"He offered to give me advice, but after reading my work, he decided that working with me on a co-author project might be a good idea." The moment the words left her lips, she regretted them. "You can't repeat that. Okay?"

"We won't breathe a word," Tayla said.

"I have to admit, I'm a little shocked that he'd consider co-writing again after what happened with Kacey," Gael said. "He told me that he didn't think he could ever trust anyone again and that's something he has issues with anyway."

Oh. If Gael only knew the things that had been happening at this campsite.

"Why?"

"Because of who he is," Gael said. "He honestly believes anyone whom he meets either wants him for his money or what he can do for their career. And women have been proving him right most of his life. And then there's his mother. She wants him married and with a kid in the worst way."

This was more information than Tiki wanted. She and Lake had agreed, their sexual relationship would come to an end soon. It had to if they were going to make working together a thing. Not only that, but Tiki didn't want to be involved with anyone. Her emotions were still raw from her breakup with Josh.

That entire thought made her want to burst out laughing. She and Lake didn't have any kind of relationship. Not romantic or working. They had no contract and even the book outline they'd been collaborating on was still so rough it could go in a million directions.

"So, I can take what he says at face value." That was the only question she really needed answered. She wasn't sure if she wanted to continue pursuing anything at all with Lake, but she didn't want to burn bridges. Lake could be a great asset in her career.

Wow. Her pulse increased. Thinking about writing as her future had been more of a fantasy.

Not a reality.

"You can trust him, if that's what you're asking," Gael said.

"What aren't you telling her?" Tayla asked. "Because it sounds to me like there is something off about this man."

"Not off," Gael said. "He's a stand-up guy."

"But?" Tiki asked.

Gael sighed. "While I absolutely know he'd never harass or assault a woman, he is a bit of a player. I know this because I was kind of one too and we traveled in the same circle."

"Player and womanizer are interchangeable terms," Tiki said. "Not that people can't change."

"Thanks, because I'm not the same man I was before I met your sister," Gael said.

Tiki swung her legs over the side of the bench and sat up taller. The sun hung high in the bright blue sky. Boats zoomed through the channel. One pulled a tube with screaming kids, laughing and calling for the driver to go faster.

"And Lake isn't a bad person; he's just not capable of being in a monogamous relationship, and I'd hate to see you get hurt after everything that happened with Josh," Gael said.

"Thanks. I appreciate the warning, but I'm only interested in how he can help my writing aspirations and if he's trustworthy or just trying to get into my pants."

Gael laughed. "Well, he wouldn't ever use his position as an editor for that. Or as a Grant. He's often lied about who he is or what he does when it comes to women."

Now that didn't surprise her.

"I'll see you two in a few days." She ended the call. Relaxing her shoulders, she sucked in a deep breath. The only thing she needed to do now was make sure Lake understood that there would be no more sex. She hadn't wanted to believe the story about his affair with his ex-girlfriend Sarah Winslow who was dating some guy by the name of Paolo Diez, but now she wondered if that was true.

She tried not to judge him since he wasn't the one cheating and that was on Sarah, but he knew she was in a relationship and that made him guilty in her eyes.

Tiki wouldn't bring it up, but she would set boundaries and ask for some kind of contract to protect her professional interests.

9

Normally, Lake loved waking up alone. He certainly preferred having the bed to himself on a regular basis. He had to admit that he and Tiki needed a break from each other. The intense heat between them had become unbearable and almost impossible to work through.

Well, that wasn't entirely true.

He thrived on the chemistry.

But that kind of sexual mixture wouldn't last forever. He'd seen it with his mother's friends in Hollywood and in New York City. Actors and actresses felt that magical connection on stage and in front of the camera. They fed off the emotions of their characters. The drama they were playacting became real. They became involved in a steamy love affair that crashed and burned when either a new project started or something shinier came along.

However, this wasn't that.

Lake scratched the scruffy growth on the side of his face and concentrated on her manuscript, *Her Stolen Memory*, the working title they had come up with last night while toasting marshmallows. He had to admit it was fantastic. She'd really taken his advice and put it to good work. Her edits went way beyond what he expected.

The additional chapter was even better. He couldn't wait to read more. He was literally salivating.

Then he remembered how she'd asked him for a contract for their collaboration.

She wanted it today.

It made sense and he would provide her with a fair one that protected them both.

Only he wondered where the desire for one came from and why she was suddenly so distant. She hadn't even kissed him goodnight. She'd been so cold that it made him shiver. When he pressed, she waggled her finger in his direction, reminding him of their conversation and how he didn't do relationships and how they were simply ridding themselves of the tension.

She kicked up her heels and declared it gone.

He declared it bullshit—but only to himself.

He shifted. His stomach growled and his head pounded from not sucking down enough caffeine. He glanced at his cell, which desperately needed a charge.

So did his computer.

It was almost noon and he wasn't going to be able to hide in his tent all day like a toddler even though he wanted to.

It wasn't like he'd never been rejected before. It happened. However, because of who he was, he had a few lady friends he called.

Friends with benefits.

Women who wanted the same thing. A physical partnership without the strings and they certainly didn't want to be in the tabloids. It was just sex.

He sighed. After being with Tiki, he realized he hadn't been having very good sex lately. It hadn't been bad. Just not the kind of sex that kept him wanting to come back for more.

Or tied up his mind for hours.

Damn. He had to find a way to get this girl out of his head.

He pulled up the contract that he'd asked his

assistant to send over. This should for sure kill the mood.

Gretchen was in the Bahamas and would be for the next couple of weeks, enjoying her vacation. She had been a loyal employee for the last three years, even though rumors continued to pop up about her friendship with Kacey. Every time they did, Lake had Tag research them. It was always random.

But something didn't settle right lately.

It wasn't that he didn't trust Gretchen. He did.

It was Kacey who was the rat.

He had hired Gretchen before the Kacey incident. He hadn't known about their close friendship until someone else pointed it out. When the shit hit the fan, Gretchen chose Grant Publishing and the truth. The thing he liked the most about Gretchen was that she kept her personal life out of work. If there was drama, he didn't know about it. And she was willing to make her vacation all about him. She actually loved the idea and couldn't wait to travel back to the Bahamas every year.

Not many people would do that.

She also didn't ask too many questions, but this time she responded with half a dozen.

Why do you want a co-author contract?
Are you planning on trying again?

If so, with who?

And are you crazy after the last time?

Why do you want a generic contract and not one from Grant Publishing?

Do you plan on leaving Grant Publishing? Because you can't edit for Grant Publishing and publish a novel with a different publisher. That would be a conflict of interest.

Well, duh. He knew that. What surprised him was that she didn't ask why he was emailing from a personal account and not his company email. The last thing he needed was for his father, or anyone at Grant Publishing, to find out what he was up to. This had to be done in the vein of *ask for forgiveness later*.

He'd respond to all of Gretchen's questions—and more—later. Right now, it was time to face the music with Tiki. He stepped from his tent to find the sexy Tiki Johnson lounging in a folding chair, wearing another damn sexy bikini top and boy shorts, with her laptop on her legs and her fingers tapping away.

Her enthusiasm was contagious.

It had been a long time since he'd met anyone with her kind of innocence when it came to the world of publishing. He hated that she would eventually be tainted by the cruel realities of what lay ahead in her career.

"Good afternoon," she said without even glancing up. "If I hadn't heard you at five this morning, I might have been worried something bad happened to you. Now I'm only concerned you're avoiding me." She closed her computer and shifted. "Is there a problem?"

"Nope." He tucked his electronics under his arm. "I've been reading and working on what you sent me. It's good. Really good. You take direction incredibly well. I have some more notes on the new material." He waved his laptop. "But I'm almost out of juice and my assistant just emailed the contract you wanted. I need to look it over and make sure she made the necessary adjustments to it."

"You are all business."

He nodded. "That's what you wanted." His heart dropped to his toes and his emotions had no place to go except take over his mind where they made it difficult for him to even be around her without wanting to either go back to bed or be all about the writing.

He opted for the latter. Only he wished he could be less dry about it.

"Besides, I'm excited," he said. "I'm jazzed for your book, and I think we have a good idea for our collaboration. I want to keep the ball rolling on it, but I know you want that contract."

She set her laptop on the small table next to her and stood, tucking her hair behind her ears. "I'm sorry if I made this awkward. However, my sister worked for a ruthless designer who nearly stole—"

Lake held up his hand. "Please. You've done nothing of the sort. We should have a contract. Most business partners do and that's what we are, even if this book doesn't get picked up by Grant Publishing."

He inched closer. He smiled back and then cleared his throat. "Are you sure you're okay with killing it if my company doesn't publish it?"

"Yes," she said. "I understand you can't have your name attached to another publisher. I only ask that I be given an equal opportunity for my solo project to be seen by unbiased eyes."

"That's why I'm pushing you so hard to finish it. If we can put your novel in front of Brandi and get her to buy it, then we've got half the battle covered. If nothing else, you've started your career."

"You want your sister to be my editor?"

He nodded. "Your book is exactly the kind of novel she's looking for and I know she'll bring it to the acquisitions meeting. Trust me." With his free hand, he gripped her hip and drew her close, brushing his lips over her mouth, slipping his tongue inside and twirling it around hers in a seductive dance. "I missed you last night," he whispered.

"Lake. We can't do this," she said.

He pressed his finger over her lips. "You're an incredible woman and I don't want whatever this is between us to end yet."

She dropped her hands and took a step back.

He took her hand and kissed it. "Don't make me beg."

"As much as I'd like to see that, I feel like now that we've entered the contract part of our partnership and helping me get a book finished to submit to your sister, tossing sex into the mix is only going to derail us both."

"I would agree with that statement if we were anywhere but this island."

She patted the center of his chest. "I agreed this would be a one-time thing. I don't want to be added to your long list of affairs and end up news."

He curled his fingers around her wrist. "Excuse me? What does that mean?"

"Nothing, really."

"You don't get to say something like that to me and then tell me it was just some flippant comment," he said behind a tight jaw. "Where did that come from?"

"I understand that you want to keep your private life exactly that. I want that too. I just came off a bad breakup and the last thing I need is anyone judging me for a fling, which is what this was—no offense."

"None taken," he said. "But how does that equate to an affair that becomes news?" He set his laptop on the chair, folded his arms, and glared. "And what's with the harsh tone?"

She made a scoffing sound, something he'd heard before.

From his mother.

Every time he landed in the tabloids for something he didn't do.

He took Tiki by the forearms, catching her gaze. "Talk to me."

She sucked in a deep breath and sighed. "I saw the article about you and your ex-girlfriend."

"Which article? There are so many." He shook his head in disgust. Of course she Googled him. Every woman he ever met had. Why would she be any different? "Which ex and what lie or fabrication are we discussing?" Though, he could gander a guess.

Tiki cocked her head and pursed her lips. "Sarah."

Perhaps his mother was right and he should have made a statement.

"You shouldn't believe everything you read," he said.

"Not even the point." She glanced toward the lake.

He followed her gaze.

A fishing boat drifted by the dock. Two men sat on the bench behind the wheel, sipping coffee and staring at their lines. One had a phone in his hands.

Lake didn't like that, but what could he do?

Besides be paranoid.

"I don't want to be Sarah. Ever. It doesn't matter to me if you and she are still having fun between the sheets every once in a while."

"Stop right there," he said with a dark tone. "I can't control the tabloids from printing lies."

"You could have made a statement that it wasn't true." She pursed her lips. "Silence speaks volumes."

"I can't help it if people read shit into my lack of words, and for the record, Sarah and Paolo didn't want me to. They didn't want any more attention brought to the entire ugly scene and because they are *both* my friends, I will respect their wishes, regardless of what people think of me."

Tiki stood there with her mouth gaping open. She said nothing. She didn't even gasp.

He should snag his computer, turn on his heel, and let her stew in that crap for a long moment, but he opted to wait for her to collect her thoughts, which only took a few seconds.

"I'm sorry that I jumped to the wrong conclusion," she said.

"Apology accepted. But I don't think that story is what has you mad."

"Actually, it's exactly that headline that got to me." She cocked her head and had that steely-eyed look about her. One that reminded him that she'd had her heart ripped from her chest. "Josh cheated on me and it wasn't a one-time thing. Even after he called it off with Jules while we tried to work things out, he still talked to her. Confided in her behind my back." Tiki waved her hand. "I understand when I broke up with him that he could see whomever he wanted—including her—but when he and I decided to give us a second chance, he should have stopped seeing her, but he didn't."

"I'm sorry he hurt you." Lake wanted to wrap his arms around her and kiss away the pain. "But I'm not him and I respect Paolo—who happens to be a good friend of mine—and there is nothing between me and Sarah. Hasn't been in years. Paolo knows that."

Tiki closed her eyes and lowered her head. "It's hard enough to deal with that kind of thing privately. I can't imagine doing it in the public eye."

"You learn to ignore it, but when people you care about start believing the stories, that's when it gets hard." He ran his hands up and down her arms.

Her lashes fluttered, showing her vulnerable gaze. "I am sorry."

"It's okay. But next time, ask me. I'll be honest with you. I have no reason to lie."

She nodded.

"Now, are you seriously going to keep shutting me down? Because I thought that while we were here, on this island, in our own little world where no one would ever know, we could enjoy each other." He dared to kiss her strawberry lips. "I was hoping we'd be able to balance work and pleasure for the short time we have our privacy intact."

"Are you sure about the privacy part? I don't want to become part of some gossip column."

"You Googled me, right?"

She nodded.

"And where did the tabloids say I went on vacation?"

"The Bahamas where there has been one sighting of you with some tall redhead."

"See, you can't believe everything you read." He laughed. "So? Can we sleep in the same tent tonight? Or maybe have a little afternoon delight?"

"That sounds intriguing." She wrapped her arms around his shoulders. "I suppose I could take a little time out of my busy writing schedule for some guilty pleasures."

"Is that what I am?"

"Yes," she said with a throaty groan. "But we can't let this get out of hand. Work comes first. We set our daily goals and no hanky-panky until those are achieved. Deal?"

"I think I can handle that." The reality was that once his vacation was over, they didn't have to see each other.

He rarely saw any of his authors with the exception of a few award ceremonies or the occasional conference and that was once or twice a year. And only his top authors.

She wouldn't be one of his and even with them working together, they didn't have to be in the same room to make magic. He knew three other writing pairs who wrote together but almost never spent any time in the same room.

"Balance would have to be the key word and that's not something we've managed so far." He kissed her nose.

"How about we work until seven, and then we take a break for a good dinner, some wine, and a little night cap." She winked. "If you know what I mean."

"Only if you agree that we need to wake early and get the pleasure out of the way."

She groaned. "You drive a hard bargain." She raised up on tiptoe and kissed him with purpose.

There was no turning back now. For as long as she was his neighbor on this campsite, he would be doing whatever she wanted. Perhaps not the best business decision he'd ever made; however, soon enough he'd be able to put his head on straight and focus on the task at hand.

Not the woman in his arms.

He broke the intense passion and held her at arm's length with his hands gripping her hips. "I need to charge my computer and get you that contract."

"And I have a goal of five thousand words by dinner."

"If anyone can do it, you can." He smiled. "Send me your next chapter before you get too far. We can keep going that way so you can stay on track with plotting. That's where you tend to derail yourself."

"So you keep telling me."

"Trust me. This isn't my first rodeo."

She rolled her eyes. "Yes, Yoda."

He laughed as he reached around her and snagged his laptop. Turning, he paused midstep. That damn fishing boat was pulling away. That shouldn't be a problem, except he didn't think they'd been there all that long. Shit like that always made him nervous. For years, he used to rent a cabin up in Lake Placid until someone figured it out, took pictures of him, and sold them to the tabloids.

That could easily happen here.

He let out a long breath. He chalked it up to nerves and the fact that he had his head in the gutter.

∽

Tiki stretched and blinked open her eyes. "What are you doing?"

"Getting a head start on the day," Lake said. He snuggled up behind her, his hand gliding up and down her bare thigh. "It's nearly five thirty and I don't want you to get behind on your words, especially after I sent you back all my notes."

"I'm glad you're not going to be my editor," she managed between ragged breaths.

He quickly removed her panties. His fingers gently danced across her hard nub, dipping inside her, and then repeating the motion, teasing her, something he enjoyed way too much.

Not that she was complaining.

His other hand unclasped her bra and cupped her breast. He pinched her nipple, gently at first.

"I'll be much tougher on you as your writing partner," he whispered in her ear.

"Is that a promise?" Arching her back, she put pressure where she knew it would be most effective.

He groaned.

She'd had her share of boyfriends over the years, but she'd never been promiscuous. She'd always been careful about her choice in bed partners. Lake had been the first man in years for whom she'd tossed caution to the wind. She told herself it was purely physical. The emotions she felt brewing below the surface were there only because of the orgasms he'd provided. Each lovemaking session had left her breathless and wanting more. She'd been thoroughly satisfied, but her body and mind knew with each gentle touch, tender kiss, or smoldering gaze what Lake could provide.

And only Lake.

It was as if he'd ruined her for any other potential lovers.

That might have been a dramatic response and in the long run, she'd get over it—and him.

"If you want it to be, yes." He kissed her neck, rolling her to her back, making his way toward her naked breasts. "Whatever you want, I'll give it to you. Both in pleasure and in work."

"How is it that you manage to make everything sound sexy?"

He didn't answer with words. Instead, he twisted her nipples and nestled his head between her legs.

She gasped, digging her fingers into his scalp. She breathed deeply, but her lungs never fully filled with oxygen. Her toes curled. Her skin ignited. Fire raced through her veins. It was as if an explosion had gone off inside her body and the only one who could contain the complete destruction was Lake.

Slamming her heels into the air mattress, she rolled her hips. The tent spun. Her vision blurred and her climax hit her system like a runaway freight train.

"I could get used to starting every day like that," he mused.

"You won't hear me complaining," she said. "But we're not done yet."

"I was hoping you'd say that."

She took him in her hands and smiled.

He shuddered.

While they really didn't know each other all that well, it seemed they never had a lack of understanding each other's needs sexually. There had been a little guiding here and there in the beginning, but nothing awkward.

Nothing like she'd experienced with—she wouldn't even think his name.

He didn't matter anymore.

Only Lake.

"You're killing me," Lake said. "Enough of that. I have to have you." He didn't give her a chance to reply. He rolled on top of her and thrust himself inside her while kissing her passionately. It was tender and wild and everything she'd ever fantasized about.

Fireworks went off inside her body. Or maybe it was a lightning storm with a dozen flashes of electricity followed by thunderous claps.

Every muscle burned with desire.

He called out her name as his climax spilled into her with such force she felt as though a hurricane had landed.

She wrapped her arms and legs around him and did her best to catch her breath, but she wondered if that would ever be possible again.

She didn't want to think about Josh and really, she wasn't, except for one thought.

She hadn't loved him. Not for a long time. She had been holding on to the thought of love. And the fact she didn't like to fail.

At anything.

Including love.

Especially love.

She ran her fingers up and down Lake's back, using her nails where she knew he liked it most.

"Mmmmmm. That feels so good." He lifted his head, fanning her cheeks with his thumbs. "You're so beautiful."

"You're sweet."

"I have my moments, but that's just the truth and not just on the outside. You're a special woman. Don't ever let anyone tell you otherwise."

She palmed his face. "I might hate myself for asking this, but are you always this—"

"No." He rolled to the side, pulling the sleeping bag over their bodies. He reached for his cell.

"Wow. That's harsh."

"Sorry. I didn't mean for it to be. But I don't dish out compliments, especially like that. However, you really are one of a kind." He turned and smiled, waving his phone. "I never did charge it yesterday."

"Do you need to make a call?" She winked, knowing one, it was too early. And two, he only needed it to check his email, which he did frequently. In the few days she'd known him, she'd learned that his vacations weren't that at all. He used them to write, but he also kept in close contact with his parents, his sister, and his assistant, Gretchen.

Tiki had yet to have any communication with Gretchen, but she'd heard a fair amount about the girl who took one for the team three years in a row. He trusted Gretchen with both his location and his current plans; therefore, she had to trust her as well.

"Aren't you cute this morning?" He tapped her nose. "But I do need to reach out to my parents sometime today. My mom has a big announcement and I need to know what that's going to look like."

"What kind of an announcement? If you don't mind me asking." She found one of his shirts and boxer shorts and put them on. They were so much more comfortable than her pajamas. She might have to steal a pair.

She inwardly laughed. She did that once with a young man she had a huge crush on in college. They never dated, but she snagged his hockey jersey and never gave it back.

He propped himself up on his elbow and stared deep into her eyes. "I suppose I can tell you. It's not like you're going to go running off and scoop her big news."

"Nope and since I didn't charge my phone last night either, I bet it's dead too."

He chuckled. "My mom's been offered to play Lilly's mom in *A Girl Named Lilly,* which is the movie she won an Oscar for back when she was a teenager."

"You're kidding. That's amazing." Tiki tucked her hair behind her ears and sat crisscrossed. She rested her hand on Lake's chest. "My sisters and I have seen that movie half a dozen times. It's one of our favorite classics."

"Are you serious?"

"Oh yes," she said. "Who did they get to reprise the role your mom originally had as Lilly?"

"Jennifer Allen."

"Wow. She's like one of the hottest actresses in Hollywood. Have you ever met her before?"

"I haven't. But my mother has." He pushed himself to a sitting position. "And sadly, I wouldn't put it past her to try to fix me up, even if I've told her a million times not to." He shook his head. "She did that with Katrina Watson. What a nightmare."

"Oh. My. God. I remember that. You and she were like a huge deal."

"No. We were not. That was all a stunt driven by my mom when she was in a made-for-television movie with Katrina. I would go to my favorite coffee shop in the morning on my way to work and I'd run into Katrina. No big deal, but then the next thing I'd know, a picture of us chatting would show up in some tabloid with a stupid headline about are they or aren't they a couple. My mom would feed her my schedule and invite her over to the house for family dinners. It was insane. But it backfired in the worst way and totally embarrassed the family."

"I kind of remember that too." She tapped her temple. She didn't normally follow these kinds of stories, but Tayla had been working with a designer who was supplying the clothes for the movie. "Something about an email getting out between

Katrina and your mom and money had been exchanged."

"It was so embarrassing," Lake said. "And it took a long time for me to trust my mother again. Which I do. Sort of. I mean, she has a singular focus when it comes to me and women, and we are definitely not on the same page."

"She wants her son to be married and have a bunch of babies?"

Tiki couldn't mistake the misery in Lake's eyes, only she couldn't tell where the pain came from.

"I don't like breaking my mother's heart, but it's never going to happen. She should focus more on Brandi, who does want to get married and have kids."

Tiki wanted to ask him why, but deep down, she didn't want to know the answer. That would be too real. It was best for her own heart if she didn't. The only thing she needed to know was that they were not a match and this drove that point home.

"Ever?" Shit. That opened pandora's box.

"That's correct."

"When I was younger, I didn't give having a family much thought. My younger sister, Tonya, was all about getting married and having children. She's a wedding planner."

"Good business to be in if you're a romantic."

Tiki agreed. "Tayla had goals that included a husband and kids, but she got sidetracked."

"She's the one engaged to Gael?"

"They're getting married in a couple of weeks and they've mentioned having kids," Tiki said. "But I was the one who everyone thought would be the last one to be tied down. I was so fickle when I was younger and I had no direction until I landed as a paralegal and then met Josh."

"Your ex—the asshole."

"That's one way to describe him."

"In my opinion, the only way."

She wouldn't argue that point. "Anyway. I used to believe that I didn't care about marriage or kids. But I know now that's not true."

He leaned in and gave her a sweet kiss. "I hope you get everything you desire."

There was no point continuing this conversation. He'd made up his mind and he wasn't the one for her anyway. There was no reason for her to be upset. This was a fling. She'd helped set the boundaries. She had no right thinking it could be more.

"I'm not in a hurry," she said, which was true. "Right now, my life is all about a new career and making sure I don't have to move back in with Mommy and Daddy."

He arched a brow. "Things are that bad?"

"Well, I'm unemployed and while I have a savings account, it isn't much, and I don't want to dip into it, so yeah. I only have a couple of months before I need to find a steady job or consider a different living arrangement." She covered her mouth with her hand. She didn't want to hear any ideas he might have or offers of financial resources. "My sister Tayla is having lunch with a friend of hers who is a private investigator who might need help in her office. That would be a good job for me. I also rent my carriage house from a state trooper and he might know of something as well. I'll land on my feet. I'm not worried."

"I was going to suggest ghost writing or maybe taking a test at my office to read through slush piles."

She shook her head. "I think that could end up being a conflict of interest if we work together."

"You could be right." He pushed back the covers and jumped to a standing position, finding a pair of jeans and a T-shirt. "I'm going to take my electronics down to the boat to charge. Shall I take yours as well?"

"You can take my phone, but my computer is at

one-hundred percent," she said. "I'll put on a pot of coffee and start some oatmeal while I get crackin' on some words."

"Sounds like a perfect plan." He leaned over and brushed his mouth over hers as if it were a normal thing to do.

A boyfriend thing to do.

But it wasn't. It was simply what they were doing for the next few days, and then it was over.

Shit. That was the last thing she wanted. But if their working partnership was going to be successful, she had to step away.

"Um, Tiki. We have company."

10

Lake sat at the table and palmed his mug of coffee. He brought it to his lips and took a long slow sip. His stomach churned. His heart literally beat in the center of his throat. Every couple of seconds he felt as if he were choking on it.

He glanced around the table at his old friend Gael and his new fiancée, Tayla, as well as Tiki. He shifted his gaze back to the tablet that Gael had set up and read the headline again. *Lake Grant is not in the Bahamas! And he's working on a book. Or is he?*

He didn't bother to read the article. He didn't have to.

The photograph was as clear as day. He turned his head and quickly lowered his shades. Two boats were floating in the water about fifty feet off his dock.

They were not fishermen.

There were only three people who knew his exact location.

Himself.

Tag.

And Tiki.

Gretchen and his parents knew he was in Lake George. They knew how to reach him, but they wouldn't know how to find him if they tried. Unless they went through Tag, which was always the protocol.

As far as his co-authoring project. Well, the only people who knew he was even considering it was himself.

Gretchen.

And Tiki.

He didn't want to believe it, but Tiki was the common denominator and he'd learned the hard way in life that most things weren't random.

"How is this possible? How did I become the story?" Tiki took the tablet in her hands and used her finger to enlarge the image. "How do they even know my name? Mom and Dad have to be beside themselves. How's Grandpa taking this?"

"Not well," Gael said. "I had to fend off the old man with a broom this morning. I wouldn't be surprised if he's in his old canoe paddling his way here."

Lake aggressively set his mug on the table. Scalding coffee sloshed out, smacking his skin. He didn't flinch even though it hurt like hell. He snagged the tablet and raised it in the air, shaking it like an angry child. "You're concerned about becoming the story? Are you kidding me? This would do your career a lot of good."

"What are you talking about?" Tayla asked with a narrowed stare. "She doesn't have one and the mention of the two of you co-authoring is more of a pun to the two of you shacking up."

"Not the point." Lake set the electronic device facedown on the table. "The question is, how does anyone know where I am or that we're even considering writing together?" He stared right at Tiki.

That old cliché saying, *if looks could kill, he'd be dead*, popped into his head. Her murderous glare tore through his soul.

He swallowed.

Hard.

"What exactly are you accusing me of?" Tiki asked.

"Nothing," Lake managed. "However, that is the burning question of the hour and you know it's the thing I feared the most."

When Gael and Tayla had first shown up and told them about the story that broke late last night and how they had been trying to reach them, Lake explained who knew what and it always came back to the fact someone had to have betrayed his trust.

"That picture was taken yesterday," Tiki said. "At around twelve thirty."

"How do you know?" Tayla asked.

"Because it's when Lake decided to come out of his tent. We'd had a bit of an argument," Tiki said.

"Why does any of that matter?" Lake pinched the bridge of his nose. The only good news that would come out of this was that all the attention shifted off Sarah and Paolo. But now he'd have to find a different vacation spot. He'd have to pack up his campsite and move.

Actually, he'd have to call it a day and go home.

The paparazzi could be relentless and they would fake fish off his dock all day long and there wasn't a damn thing he could do about it. If he were alone, he might tolerate them.

Tiki would be gone in a couple of days. Maybe he would stay.

But what to do about her.

"I remember while I was waiting for you to wake up that there was a fishing boat off our dock. I thought that a weird place to fish. And one of the guys always had his phone out," Tiki said. "When did you send the email about contracts to your assistant?"

"You're blaming Gretchen for this?" Lake had no reason to believe Gretchen was anything but loyal, especially after the whole Kacey thing. "She wouldn't betray me like that."

"I never said she did. I'm simply putting together a timeline." Tiki flattened her hands on the wood planks and stood. She leaned over the table. "Is it possible your email got hacked?"

He had used a Gmail account, which he gathered wouldn't have been as secure as his company one. But he'd done that to keep his parents out of the loop. "I suppose that could have happened. But I didn't write in those emails my location. Only the co-authoring part and as your sister so poignantly pointed out, the tabloids are only focused on the fact you're the latest notch on my bedpost."

Tiki gasped. She turned and stomped off. Her sister followed.

"That was rude," Gael said.

"I'm pissed off and I'm sorry, but she's the only person who could have leaked this story that makes sense." Lake raked a hand across the top of his head. "My mother's right. I always pick the worst partners to work with."

"She was only right about Kacey," Gael said. "Tiki isn't like that and I can guarantee you that there is no way in hell she went to the press. She hates being the center of attention. When she told us she was going to write a book and I mentioned how if it was successful she'd have to go out on book tours, her face turned green. I thought she might hurl right there."

The problem that Lake had now was how little he knew about Tiki. If he were to be asked twenty questions about her, he figured he might know half.

If he was lucky.

"The only other person who knows is Tag and we both know he didn't go to the tabloids."

Gael laughed. "No. He wouldn't."

"My mother's going to kill me," Lake said. "This is going to overshadow her big announcement today."

"Ah. The movie. Yeah." Gael turned his phone over. "I set up news alerts on your name and it's been going nuts all morning. It's all about you and

Tiki. Your mom hit once. And it was like an afterthought."

"Shit. This was supposed to be her moment and I've gone and made a mockery of it."

Gael shook his head. "Phoebe Grant is going on every scheduled talk show." He glanced at his watch. "Starting in fifteen minutes. She'll talk up her movie and she'll make it all about herself and barely bring any light to you and this bullshit."

"I hope you're right because I'll never hear the end of this as it is," Lake said. "My dad is not on board with me writing and publishing a novel and especially not with a co-author."

"I remember."

"The thing is, Tiki is one of the most talented, incredibly raw writers I've met in a long time. She's going to go places and I really wanted to work with her."

"Then why'd you sleep with her?" Gael asked.

That was a valid question. Lake inhaled sharply, sucking in that fresh Adirondack pine scent. He could never get that in the city. Not even in Central Park. It always managed to smell of hot dogs and exhaust.

Lake picked up his coffee mug and sipped. He needed a bolt of caffeine. He wished it had a shot of whiskey in it to help him get through the rest of the day. "What bothers me is that I like her and now I don't trust her. That sucks because I don't like that feeling when it comes to Tiki. She's special."

"Are you saying you have feelings for Tiki?" Gael leaned back and folded his arms. "Because that's not something you do."

Lake laughed. "Says the man who swore he'd never get married again."

Gael cracked a smile. His eyes twinkled like stars blanketing the dark sky. He cleared his throat. "We're not talking about me, but nice try on the deflection, and for the record, Tayla and I knew that you asked her to co-write."

"Excuse me?"

"She called us because she was concerned you weren't necessarily who you said you were or that maybe you were taking her for a ride or just trying to get her into bed. I told her about Kacey."

"So, someone could have overhead her talking."

That didn't exonerate Tiki, but it did open her up to reasonable doubt.

Maybe.

"Why didn't you tell me this sooner? Why did you let me go on being an asshole?"

"Because you're good at that," Gael said. "And

even I have to admit that it seems weird this happened. Oftentimes, it is those who are the closest to us."

"You're referring to Gretchen," Lake said.

"She was friends with Kacey."

"Was being the operative word." Lake had heard it all before, especially since he kept Gretchen on after the scandal. But she'd been there for him through it all. Even when he thought he was going to lose the battle. "And once the story started to turn, Gretchen knew to distance herself from Kacey."

"Maybe. But while you think Tiki is the one with the knowledge and therefore the power and possibly the one behind this, then explain why the facts of her life are so limited."

"Because she planted it."

"You really think she's that diabolical?" Gael asked. "Anyone who wanted a story like that to leak to better position themselves would do everything in their power to at least make themselves look good in the public eye. This article does not."

Lake lifted the tablet and read the story again, focusing this time on the details surrounding Tiki.

It mentioned her name.

A nobody-wannabe writer looking for a payday

willing to sleep her way to the top and Lake was all too willing to do it.

But it was what came next that sucker punched him right in the gut.

The leaked email to Gretchen.

It was fake. Well, sort of. He had sent one from that account, asking for a contract, but the correspondence was wrong. In his original email he asked Gretchen to use discretion. That he wasn't ready to share with his father what he was doing. She asked her litany of questions and he responded. But what was leaked to the press was something very different.

It a nutshell, Lake demanded that a contract from his publishing house be drawn up between him and Tiki for a co-authoring project. That it was a done deal. Period.

That's not what happened.

"Fuck," he mumbled. "I hadn't read all of that."

"I didn't think so and I don't think Tiki got to that part either." Gael glanced over his shoulder. "I'm sure Tayla is informing her of the true ugliness of it all."

"None of it's true and I'm going to have to go back to New York and issue a statement."

Gael clasped his hands together and leaned forward. "You also have to find a way to save Tiki's career. She hasn't even had a chance to get it off the ground and I know having a book published is important to her."

"That will be the easy part," Lake said. "If the fallout of this is too much for my sister to take on, I'll make sure someone else signs her. Trust me. She's got what it takes. However, we need to deal with this problem first."

"Thank you for be rational about this."

"Oh. I might still freak out." Lake took in a long cleansing breath. He still struggled with his emotions. He couldn't fathom Tiki sending this to the press. The only thing it did was destroy her chances of a career without the kind of controversy that questioned her talent.

Gretchen had no reason for doing it all.

Who did that leave and how did they get the intel?

Anyone who wanted a payday.

"Your mom is about to go on air. Shall we watch?" Gael asked.

Lake nodded. He quickly stole a glance at his cell. He was shocked that neither his parents nor even legal had tried to contact him yet. Gretchen, on the other hand, had been blowing up his phone. He chose to ignore her for the time being.

"Hey, Tayla and Tiki. We're going to watch Phoebe on the morning show. Are you two going to join us?" Gael asked.

"Be right there," Tayla said.

"What do you think they have been talking about?" Lake asked.

"I wouldn't dare take a guess at that, but I doubt it's positive when it comes to you."

"I deserve that," Lake said.

"You absolutely do."

Tiki and her sister rejoined them at the picnic table, Tiki on one side of Gael and Tayla on the other side.

That was fine with Lake. He stood behind them so he could see the screen. A breeze flowed in off the water, carrying Tiki's strawberry shampoo with it.

Inwardly, he moaned.

"Turn it up," he said as the show cut back from the commercial. His mother often had a flair for the dramatic when it came to her entrances. But not this time. No. Instead, she sat on a stool wearing a cool summer dress, with her sleek hair and big smile.

"Welcome back, everyone," Gigi, the host, said. *"I'm so excited to be sitting here with Phoebe Grant, who won an Oscar for her role as Lilly in* A Girl Named Lilly *when she was only seventeen years old. She's now going*

to be playing Lilly's mother, Annabel, in the reboot. Welcome, Phoebe."

"Thank you so much for having me," his mother said.

"Now, we all saw the headlines this morning and I'd be doing my audience a grave disservice if I didn't ask you about that article regarding your son, Lake."

His mom nodded and held up her hand. "I understand, Gigi."

"This is staged," Lake whispered. "My mom rehearsed this with Gigi."

"How do you know?" Tiki glanced over her shoulder.

"Because she's not acting shocked, indignant, or refusing to answer."

"Neither Lake, his writing partner, his sister Brandi, nor my husband had wanted this to come out yet," his mother said.

"What the..." Lake let the superlative linger on his tongue like a piece of candy.

"Are you saying that Lake and the young woman whom he was spotted with in a lip-lock is his co-author in a book?" Gigi asked.

His mother smiled. "I cannot discuss the details. But I can tell you that my husband and I are so proud of our son. And we're super excited for him."

"What about the rumors about him and his ex-girl—"

His mother waved her hand. "Gigi. Those were rumors and that picture that has been circulating this morning clearly puts that to rest. Like I said. Chandler and I couldn't be happier for our son. Now let's talk about A Girl Named Lilly, *shall we?"*

"Turn it off," Lake said. He turned and strolled toward the water. He stared at the boats floating. There were three. All had tossed at least one fishing line over the side, but he knew they were only fishing for a story.

One man actually stood up with his cell in hand.

Lake smiled and waved, giving them what they came for.

"What the hell just happened?" Tiki asked as she approached, standing awfully close.

"Well. My mother may have forced my father's hand in letting me write a book, which I'm not sure why she did that. She's never been on board with it," Lake said. "But in doing so, she might have created a different problem for your solo career." He rubbed the back of his neck. He'd have to get with his marketing team on how to deal with that. And he would just as soon as he got back to the city. No way would he let Tiki's talents be wasted on only co-writing with him and he felt like if her first book was the one they did together, it would screw her.

He didn't care if that was what he got pigeonholed into because he'd always have his career as a publisher to fall back on.

"She also left it hanging what we are to each other," Lake said. "That concerns me the most. The press could come full tilt."

Tiki placed her hand over her eyes, shielding them from the sun. "They're taking pictures of us, aren't they."

"A few."

Under normal circumstances he wouldn't be giving the paparazzi anything to shoot and he'd be telling her to take cover. But there was nothing normal about this. He had no idea what to do or how to handle it, other than he'd let Tiki call a few of the shots.

"If you want to kill the story, we can do it now," he said.

"You mean end the book partnership?"

"No." He turned. "I think we make sure that moves forward. However, we need to talk to a few people, my father for one, and make sure you are protected."

"Thank you for that."

He nodded.

"But I'm talking about the questions that every reporter wants to know and what the ones in the boats are trying to be the first to break," he said.

"Oh," she whispered. "You're referring to us romantically."

"We can play this a couple of different ways."

"I don't want to play it at all," she said. "I don't want to be in this situation. Can we make them go away?"

"No." He sighed. "They are in open waters, fifty feet away from the dock. They aren't doing anything illegal. We can, however, take this conversation inside the tent." He took her by the hand and tugged. "We'll be back shortly." He unzipped his tent and followed her inside.

He flopped on the air mattress and clasped his hands behind his head.

She opted to sit on the corner. "For the record, I didn't leak anything."

"I believe you," he said. And he meant it. He'd have Tag figure out how this mess got out in the public. "I'm sorry I was a jerk."

"I can sort of understand why, but moving forward, I will struggle to trust your assistant."

He opened his eyes wide. "I don't think she's

responsible." Gretchen had been his right hand for three years. He didn't do anything without her by his side. He couldn't imagine doing this without her either. But if Tiki needed Gretchen to be sidelined, then so be it. "However, I will have my private investigator look into her more closely."

"You would do that for me?"

He nodded.

"Thank you," Tiki said. "But going back to this position your mother put us in about being a couple. I don't like it and I won't pretend."

"Five minutes ago, if I had taken you into my arms and kissed you, it wouldn't have been fake. Or for a show. I would have meant it."

"Are you kidding me right now? It absolutely would have been for effect, even if it was real. And don't go trying to tell me or anyone else something different."

She had a valid point and he wasn't about to argue with her about it either. "What do you want to do?"

"I don't know," she said. "Part of me wants to pack up and go home right now."

"I wouldn't stop you if that's what you want."

"Oh, my God. You're not helping at all," she said.

He propped himself up on his elbows. "Do you want to know what I think we should do?"

She nodded.

"In my humble opinion, I believe the only option that makes the most sense is to stay here until your reservation is completed. Then we both pack up and you come to New York City with me."

"Why would I do that?"

"To meet Brandi. To also have a sit-down with my father and legal to sign all contracts. I also want to find you a good agent. I have a few in mind."

"Is this all really happening?" She sighed, lying down on the bed. "Am I really getting a book deal?"

"It could still go sideways," he said. "You do need to prepare yourself for that."

The sound of footsteps on the platform caught his attention. "Hey, Lake. We've got a problem," Gael's voice carried through the nylon.

"What's that?" Lake pushed himself to a sitting position.

"Six more boats have shown up." Gael stuck his head inside the tent. "Tayla thinks we should call Tiki's landlord."

"Why?" Lake asked.

"He's a state trooper and also head of the Lake George Patrol," Tiki said.

"I'm also thinking it's probably best if we shut this camp down," Gael said. "It's going to make people nervous."

"No." Lake shook his head. "They will follow me. Us. It will be a nightmare. We need to find a way to get us off the island without anyone knowing. We can break down camp later."

"I've got an idea," Gael said. "You two hang tight."

"What the hell have I gotten myself into," Tiki muttered.

"Hopefully a run at the *New York Times* Best Sellers list."

11

Lake didn't like bringing other people into the fold. He hated giving up control. But the longer they stayed on this island, the worse things were going to get. Two more articles about him and Tiki had already surfaced, with more recent pictures. They weren't bad; however, the focus had turned on Tiki and who she was, and they had to get in front of that.

Tiki wasn't going to like what Lake had in mind.

He tapped his cell and prayed this time his father answered as he paced by the tree line. He knew the paparazzi could see him and they would take their pictures. Jared, the state trooper whom Tiki and her sister had called to come run interference, did as much as he legally could. He and his patrol actually cited three for not having a fishing license. However, that didn't stop them from taking pictures.

Jared did threaten a few with harassment charges, so he was making some noise and they were back down to three boats. It was more manageable but still made Lake crazy.

"Son," his dad said. "I'm sorry that I haven't responded. It's been a very hectic day and I've been putting out fires left and right."

"What the hell does that mean? And why isn't Brandi picking up either?"

"It means I've been dealing with day-to-day business stuff and your sister is right here, but she's on a call. I've been fending off reporters, giving our legal team a chance to look at everything. I'm trying not to get into it with your mother while looking into where this all came from," his father said.

"Not to state the obvious, but you should have answered my call an hour ago to discuss this and we could examine it together."

"Have you spoken to Tag?"

"Yes," Lake said. "Thank you for getting in touch with him the second the story broke."

"You're welcome. Since that call, Tag had one of his tech buddies come to the office to look into our system to see if maybe our servers were compromised and they have been."

"Dad, I sent Gretchen those emails from a personal Gmail account."

"Shit. Okay. Sorry, but you need to give this tech guy access to that then too," his father said.

"I can do that."

"Good. Now do you have any ideas on how your location was leaked to the press and care to shed light on what is true about this situation, what isn't, and what I actually have to follow through with?"

Lake's heart free-fell from the center of his chest to his ankles. His father swore he'd never cave when it came to Lake's desire to be a novelist. He had his reasons and even Lake admitted some were valid.

But most were based in fear.

Lake cleared his throat. This was an opportunity he wasn't going to pass on. His father could take it back. He could also be bullshitting him, but the door had been opened a crack. Time to state his intentions. "Well, it looks like I'm finally writing a book that will be published and we have a new author. And Dad, she's really good. I mean, we haven't seen this level good in years. Her writing is fresh and raw and you won't be able to put it down. I can send you her partial. You will be totally blown away. It will be the best debut novel of the decade. Award winning."

"Are you sure Brandi is the best editor for her?"

"Yes. But obviously Brandi has to make that call and if she doesn't want to take it on, then maybe Mark. But Dad, we can't pass on her because of this. That would be wrong."

"I agree. But you won't be able to have anything to do with her solo novel. You can't attend marketing meetings or anything," his father said with a matter-of-fact tone.

"No shit. That would be a conflict of interest." But he would be able to give Tiki advice on the side.

"The fact you let control go so quickly tells me you have slept with this girl." His dad let out a long sigh. "So, that part is actually true."

"None of your business."

"Oh. When you mix your ink in our author well, it's always my business."

"Dad. That's the worst fucking pun ever and since when have I done that? Um. Never. Not once. And until Mom let this cat out of the bag, she wasn't our author."

"Is she really that good?" his dad asked. "And I mean as a writer. Not in bed."

Lake rolled his eyes. "That's gross, Dad. Even for

you, but yeah. She writes characters like I've never seen. When I read her first chapter, which she'd literally just written like in front of me, it was spectacular. I barely had notes for her and the few I did have she was able to execute like a pro. She's a little raw with the plotting, but I've been working with her and if you continue with the bedroom jokes, I'm hanging up."

"Okay. I'll stop harassing you," his father said. "But we have to find the leak, if it wasn't this Tiki girl."

"I don't believe Tiki would do it. When I think through everything, exposing this could have shut things down."

"In part, that's why I'm trusting you that she's our next big star and signing her. Based on what Tag has told me about her, I can't see such a green writer who has been through what she has in the last month putting herself in the middle of a scandal."

"So, I'm getting to co-author a book not because you think I have any talent, but because—"

"Son, I'm going to be honest; that deal could still be killed."

"Even with Dad agreeing to let me steer this ship," Brandi's voice came over the phone. "He's got some valid points about why that might have to happen."

"That's not fair. What we're writing is complete fiction. It will be nothing like what Grandpa did. I would never bring that kind of shame on Grant Publishing or on our family."

"I know," his father said. "And this isn't about your grandfather's book. It's about how to deal with a debut author and you having never published a book. Even if this entire thing dies down before her book comes out and people forget, Google doesn't."

"Neither does the press," Lake added. He knew exactly where his father was headed. "And if I had a solo book?"

"I want success for you. And for her," his father said. "This is going to bring out haters and I know you believe that authors need them. That in order for a book to go viral it needs readers to love it and hate it."

"But when haters take over, it will tank and me being the face of the publishing company could destroy her career—and mine—before it starts."

"You said it, not me."

Lake rubbed his temple. "I'll do what's best for her and for Grant Publishing."

"Son. I said it could be killed. I didn't say I was

going to do it. We need to have a lot of discussions, and then I want to see what you've been working on. There are ways to spin this in our favor, especially if it's as good as you say it is."

"Tiki's going to knock it out of the park," Lake said. "She'll carry my ass."

His father laughed. "I've always admired your humility."

"I have to admit, I thought you were going to rip me a new one."

"Your sister has been sharing with me your plans for Grant Publishing. You two have some incredibly innovative ideas," his father said.

"No. Brandi does because most of them are hers."

"Thanks, big brother," Brandi said.

"I love you kids and I've always wanted what was best for both of you," his dad said. "But now we have to discuss your mother. While she's the love of my life and I would be lost without her, I know her faults and she can be relentless when she wants something, and she wants a grandchild."

"That's my cue to leave," Brandi said. "Talk to you later, Lake."

That was the last thing Lake wanted to discuss. "Dad, I'm the one who has to be willing to do that and I'm not." His heart tightened painfully. He glanced over his shoulder. He couldn't see Tiki. She was inside his tent, hopefully working on her manuscript or at the very least, not stressing too much over everything. He could admit to himself that he cared more about her than any other woman he'd been with in years. There was more to her than lived at the surface. Even after all she'd been through with Josh and losing her job, she'd given her soul so easily to him. Lake had been humbled the way Tiki's emotions flowed from her heart. She lived like she wrote. That's what made her such a fabulous author.

"Your mom believes you're falling in love with this young woman. She said she could tell by the way you kissed her in that picture. There was no arguing with her about it."

"I've known Tiki for barely a week."

"As if that has ever stopped your mom, and need I remind you that your mother and I were married three weeks after we met and that you were conceived—"

"Dad. I don't ever want to hear that story again." Lake rolled his shoulders. The only good thing from knowing any of his parents' history was that they were madly in love and had a good marriage.

"Can I ask you a question?" his father asked.

"Sure."

"I've seen a dozen pictures in the last few hours taken of you and her. All candid shots and every single one, with the exception of a couple, both of you look as though you are quite smitten with each other, so I can see where your mom is coming from."

"Are you believing tabloid stories?"

"No," his father said with a sharp tone. "I'm believing a look on my son's face that I've never seen before."

"It's a picture, taken by someone trying to make a buck."

"And you're avoiding my questions, which is telling all by itself," his father said.

His father was right, but no way would he cop to it. At least not while he had no idea what he honestly felt. He needed time to sort through all his emotions. The only thing he knew for certain was that his life was forever changed. "I can tell you that I like her," Lake admitted. "That I admire and respect her."

"Just be warned that your mom sees a woman who is worthy of you."

"Are you kidding? Mom hasn't even met her yet."

"True. But she found out that Gael Whalen is engaged to her sister," his father said. "I'm sorry, but when Tag reported to me, I did share certain things with your mother to keep her calm."

"No. It's okay. But I need to tell Tiki her family has been examined by our private investigator."

His dad laughed. "They have their own poking around our business. A woman named Katie Donovan and her business partner, Jackson Armstrong. Tag says they are good people and he's willing to do a sit-down with them. To work together to find the leak."

"All right. But first, I need to get off this island. Gael is working on a plan to do that tonight and bring me to a place where security can be controlled."

"Have you considered coming back to the city?" his father asked.

"I have and I need to think. Let's regroup in the morning, okay?"

"Sounds like a plan," his father said. "And son. Don't you ever forget that I'm proud of you and I love you."

"I love you too, Dad." He tapped the screen, turned, and sauntered back toward the tent. He stuck his head inside. "Hey. How are you holding up?"

"I'm focusing on fiction. Which as it turns out is

more normal than real life," Tiki said as she glanced up from her perch on the folding chair and makeshift desk that he'd set up next to the bed. It was a tight squeeze, but worth it to keep her hidden from the reporters. "How many boats are still out there?"

"Only a couple. Your friend Jared has scared most of them away."

"Good." She leaned back, closing the lid on her laptop. "I spoke to my parents and they have gotten a few calls asking for statements regarding our relationship."

"What has been their response?"

"No comment, for the most part, but my father got snarky once and told one reporter that they expected wedding bells and he'd be sure not to hit said reporter over the head with them."

Lake burst out laughing as he sat cross-legged on the bed.

"I'm so glad I can amuse you."

"I'm sorry, but your father sounds like my kind of guy."

"He does have a wickedly dry sense of humor," she said.

"I hope he'll be able to see the irony in the fact that my private investigator ran into yours."

"Yeah. Katie, our PI friend, told my dad you had someone looking into me—or my family." She tilted her head and arched a brow. "You have more trust issues than I do."

"I needed to know that you weren't here to either write some exposé story on me or that you weren't going to pull a Kacey, or something even bigger."

"For the last hour or so while you've been out there pacing, I've been in here contemplating putting the brakes on the entire deal, solo and coauthoring. However, I came to this island to begin a new chapter in my life."

"Nice metaphor."

She pursed her lips and shook her head as if in disgust, but her eyes twinkled. "In these last few days, I've realized that for most of my adult life, I have been doing things because I've been afraid to take chances. I was going to take Josh back, not because I loved him, but because it was what I knew. It was comfortable. I stayed with my job as a paralegal because before that I bounced around from one thing to the next because I was too afraid to do what I really wanted." She pointed to the computer. "I had one person tell me I wasn't good enough. That I didn't have what it takes. And then I had Josh in my ear telling me how hard it would be to make a career out of it. That I would be wasting my time and how the majority of writers can't make a living at their craft."

"He's not wrong about that." Lake held up his finger. "The part where most authors don't make enough to live off, but your ex is an asshole and doesn't know shit. You have to be one of the most talented authors I've ever met. My only concern now is all this insanity will taint people's opinions of your work. Not so much readers, but the industry, and sometimes that can be more important in the months leading up to the release. My dad, myself, and the marketing team need to figure out how to make sure nothing tanks your release. But we also have a year to let all this settle down, and it will."

"That's what Gael keeps telling me." She stood and climbed onto the air mattress, sprawling out on her side. "Thank you for believing in me."

"If you had sent me a cold submission, I would have been salivating over wanting to work with you." He reached out and took her chin with his thumb and forefinger. "Now I'm just salivating over you." He held her gaze, studying her facial reaction to his words.

Her pupils widened.

Her lips parted.

A slight gasp escaped.

"I told myself that I could voluntarily step away from you. I mean, I will if that's what is best for your career, but for the first time in my life since college, I find myself having entanglement feelings. When I hung up with my dad, I reminded myself that expressing them would be dangerous."

"I'm not sure I understand." She narrowed her stare, giving off a puzzled expression.

"You put the brakes on our fling because of what you thought happened with Kacey."

"That was part of it," she said.

"Now that we're going to be leaving the campsite tonight and my time in Lake George is coming to an end, I find myself not wanting whatever this is between us to be over."

"I see." She rolled to her back and closed her eyes. "That's a problem because I'm never going to compromise myself again like I did with Josh."

"What does that mean, exactly?"

"You live in New York City. You're the heir to Grant Publishing. That's not going to change. And I have no desire to ever leave my hometown. We could date and do the long-distance thing for a bit. But we both know a romantic relationship is destined to end."

He snuggled up next to her, wrapping his arm around her and pulling her close. "You're right." He pressed his lips against her temple, sealing his fate. He'd do what was best for her and in the long run, his heart.

There would be no co-authoring of a novel.

Only her solo book.

It's what was best.

For everyone.

And there would never be a them. A truth that hit him harder than he ever expected.

12

"My sister Tonya and her friend Foster are here." Tiki quickly sent a text response back to Tonya and then continued to fill her backpack with the few things she'd need until her father could come and get the rest of her things in the morning. Jared and his state trooper friends had promised to keep an eye on both boats, as well as the campsites to ensure nothing happened.

She owed Jared big. He and his wife, Ryan, had been incredibly supportive throughout her breakup with Josh.

"Who is this Foster person? A boyfriend or something?" Lake asked.

"No, and don't bring that up."

"Sounds like it's an issue," Lake said.

"Tonya's totally in love with Foster, but he doesn't see her that way. Hell, he doesn't see anyone that way. He's been through a lot and he's jaded. Reminds me of when I first met Gael."

"He certainly went through some dark times. However, I have to say, I've never seen him more relaxed, and he and Tayla make for an adorable couple."

"I agree," Tiki said. "Gael not only showed Tayla how she was on a downward spiral when it came to her career choices, but he helped her see how she'd completely sold herself to the devil for all the wrong reasons."

"Well, that's exactly what Gael had done."

Tiki's eyes burned every time she thought about all that Gael had lost. However, it was the idea that if he'd been the kind of man he was today, he would have gotten on that plane with his family and he too wouldn't be here to love her sister.

That kind of torture was the worst and everyone tried not to think about it, but it always seeped into their minds.

"It's hard to believe he could have been that selfish. He's such a sweet man and so good to my sister," Tiki said.

"I'm sure your sister brings out the best in him." Lake unzipped the tent and stuck his head out. "Where exactly did Tonya and Foster pull up?"

"Other side of the island," she said. "Campsite 20. Foster said it's directly behind this one and the couple staying there is someone he knows. Someone he took on a wedding ride on his boat last year and they are here on their anniversary, so it's cool."

"I hope he's right." He took her by the hand. "We can't turn on a flashlight, so stay close and be careful."

"I will." She grabbed his hips and focused on the ground. She blinked, hoping that would help her see, but it didn't. Thankfully, Lake's shoes had a white sole and she could see them separate from the dark earth. She followed his footsteps exactly. One right after the other.

He moved slowly and methodically. About twenty feet from their site, she stumbled on a root, smacking her head into his back. "Sorry," she whispered.

"Are you okay?"

"I'm fine." Her big toe throbbed and stung, but she'd stubbed it worse than that before. This pain would go away in minutes and wouldn't come back. It was a zinger. Nothing more.

"I see a campfire up ahead. Hopefully, we're heading to the right place." He paused and turned, taking her into his arms. "No matter what happens, I want you to know I don't regret a single thing."

Her heart hammered like a jackrabbit in the center of her chest. She felt his warm breath on her lips.

"Except perhaps not having more time with you." His mouth came down on hers hard and fast. His tongue swirled around hers in an all too familiar dance. It was slow, hot, and she didn't want it to end.

She gripped his shoulders, digging in tight. Desperation engulfed her emotions, which had been all over the place. Her heart was with Lake. There was no doubt about that. She was drawn to him in ways that filled her with both excitement and fear.

Pressing her hand on the center of his chest, she broke off the kiss. "No regrets."

His lips brushed across her forehead. "Where are we staying tonight?"

"Tiki? Is that you?" a faint female voice called.

"Yes," she whispered back. She laced her fingers through Lake's and squeezed. "We better get a move on." She scurried across the path where her sister came into sight.

Tonya waved frantically.

Tiki and Lake followed her through the next campsite and down to the dock where Foster waited for them in his old-fashioned wooden Chris-Craft boat.

Quickly, they boarded the vessel and took a seat right behind the driver.

Tonya sat next to Foster.

"Thanks for coming," Tiki said once they made it into the channel and up to speed. "I know it's late."

"No problem. I don't have any appointments tomorrow until one in the afternoon," Tonya said.

"Lake, this is my baby sister and our friend, Foster." Tiki reached out and squeezed her sister's hand.

"It's nice to meet you both," Lake said. "Sorry for the circumstances."

"We're happy to help," Foster said. "Not to make things awkward, but I'm huge fan of your mother's."

Lake laughed. "I get that a lot."

Tiki leaned back, resting her head on Lake's shoulder.

He lifted his arm and wrapped it around her body, running his hand up and down her arm.

She was a bit surprised by his public display of affection in front of her family. Not that everyone didn't know something had happened between them. If they weren't denying it in the tabloids, why do it with family.

The truly strange part was that it didn't feel uncomfortable or strange. If Josh even hugged her in front of her parents, it made her squirrelly. Of course, he never did, especially in the last year.

She'd learned that had more to do with his affair than anything else.

"I find myself now looking at all the books I read to see if your company published it and if you're the editor."

"Most of the time editors don't get any credit unless the author does so in the dedication or acknowledgments, and to be honest, I'm okay with that," Lake said. "I didn't come up with the idea. I didn't write the book. All I did was offer a few suggestions to make it better and work with the marketing team to get it to readers."

"Considering how you've helped me, I'd say you're being way too humble." Tiki tilted her head, catching his gaze. His intense eyes illuminated under the white moon.

He smiled before glancing over his shoulder. "It appears no one is following us."

"Jared would have texted me if someone was

anywhere near me," Foster said. "We've got a clean shot to my place."

"Is that where I'm crashing for the night?" Lake asked.

"You both are," Foster said. "Katie and Jackson have seen reporters at Tiki's parents' place and at Tonya's. But they wouldn't think to come to my house."

"I appreciate it," Lake said.

"Are you staying?" Tiki asked her sister. Foster was a confirmed bachelor. He lived in an A-frame house on Pilot Knob Road that he'd been remodeling for the last couple of years. Doug Tanner, a local contractor who was married to State Trooper Stacey Sutten, had been trying to get Foster to let him at least help with the project and occasionally, Foster allowed it.

But for the most part, it gave Foster something to do so he didn't have to socialize with people.

He had a loft for a bedroom and the rest of the house was—well—not really done.

His guest room was a small space in his boathouse. It was cozy and she had to admit nice and she wouldn't mind staying there. However, she suspected that Lake would get that spot to himself and she'd take the couch. He did have a cabin across the road.

Foster had tried to get his ex-wife to stay in it when she was in one of her more sober periods or in the winter months, but she hadn't taken him up on that, ever. So, he Airbnb'd it mostly in the summer months since it didn't have running water. Hikers who came in to do the trails around Buck and Black Mountains enjoyed staying there. It was very rustic, and that was putting it mildly.

"I'm going back to Mom and Dad's tonight," Tonya said. "I'll be going with Dad and Grandpa to close up your camps after Lake tells us what he wants us to do with his stuff."

"We haven't decided how long I need to stay here," Lake said. "My assistant is flying back to New York City tomorrow, but the PR team isn't sold that I should come running back. However, I don't want Tiki or any of you to be harassed by the media. I will check into a hotel somewhere and keep the focus off all of you."

"You are welcome to stay with me as long as you need. I have the boathouse and the cabin. Both are at your disposal." Foster slowed the boat as he approached his dock.

Tiki ran her hands through her windblown hair.

The bright-white half-moon hung high in the dark sky speckled with a million stars.

Foster maneuvered the vessel with ease into the boathouse.

Tonya jumped from the boat onto the wood planks, securing the bow and then the stern.

"Thanks, Tonya." Foster shut down the engines and collected their belongings. "Why don't we all go up to the main house and have a nightcap before Tonya takes off."

"I'd love a stiff drink." The boat rocked as Lake made his way onto the dock.

"You two go open a bottle of wine. We'll be right up." Tonya stretched out her hand, offering it to Tiki. "You certainly made a splash this week."

"That wasn't my intention." Tiki embraced her sister in the biggest bear hug, wiggling back and forth. "All I wanted was some peace and quiet and to have a little fun camping."

"Did you like real camping?"

Tiki laughed. "I did. But not for the same reasons I loved the Johnson way of doing it."

"He's cute." Tonya took both of Tiki's hands, swinging them back and forth. "Are you going to keep him?"

"He's not a stray cat."

"You know what I mean."

Tiki inhaled sharply. The cool evening air filled her lungs. The summer night smells of budding flowers mixing with the backdrop of the pine trees and the fresh water assaulted her nose. "It was just a fling. Two ships passing in the night. We're not meant to be anything other than maybe writing partners, if that even pans out."

Tonya cupped her chin. "Your eyes look sadder than when we picked you up after Josh stomped on your heart."

"I think maybe I am," Tiki admitted. "I told him earlier that we can't be together and that it was time to end it."

"Why?"

"Simple geography," Tiki said. "I'm never going to allow myself to be compromised again. Like I told Lake. I did it when I allowed others to tell me that pursuing a writing career was a dumb idea and again when I settled for a man who didn't truly love me, and the truth is, I didn't love Josh."

"Are you falling in love with Lake?" Tonya asked.

"I can't allow myself to go there. Sometime in the next ten years, his father is going to retire, leaving him Grant Publishing. His life is in New York City, a place that nearly destroyed our sister, and her fiancé.

While I understand if I get a book deal I'll have to make trips to the Big Apple, I don't ever want to leave Lake George. And he can't leave the city. He and I can't ever be."

"I'm sorry," Tonya said.

"Don't be. I'm still super grateful that I met him and not just for the opportunity that's being handed to me on a silver platter. But he showed me that I'm a whole person. That what happened between me and Josh doesn't define me. I'm going to be okay."

"I'm glad. And I'm being totally self-serving. It's just that for the last twenty-four hours, Foster has been animated and we watched one of Phoebe's old movies earlier. Having Lake around might bring me and Foster closer."

"If the co-authoring thing happens, Lake will still be in my life. Just not as anything other than a friend, so maybe that will still happen." Tiki hated giving her sister false hope, because she doubted Foster would ever come out of the hole he'd dug himself into after his child died. "Shall we go have that drink?"

And Tiki would allow herself one last night in Lake's arms.

13

Quietly, Lake slipped from the small bed, located his jeans, and hiked them up over his hips. He snagged his sweatshirt, tiptoed across the room, and opened the door, stepping out onto the balcony that overlooked the bay. God, he loved everything about Lake George. Even scandal felt different in these parts.

"Hi, Gretchen," he said softly. The sun had yet to show its bright rays over the mountains. "You're up early."

"Sorry. Did I wake you?"

"Nah," he lied. He sat down in the big Adirondack chair and put his feet up on the railing. He wanted this lifestyle so badly he could taste it. As he fell asleep last night, holding Tiki in his arms, he realized how little he felt like the city was his home.

Sure, it was where he lived.

But it wasn't where his heart belonged.

He always thought it was because he was doing what his parents wanted, not what he desired. His entire life he'd been living on borrowed time. He figured once his father retired, he could do what he wanted and that was to write a book. His sister promised she'd make sure it would happen, though she believed they would have to wait a few years.

He was tired of waiting.

And Tiki showed him there was more to life than a career. Whether she knew it or not, she had helped him and his family come together in ways they hadn't in years. Even his text messages with his mother had a different tone. More relaxed. Less about baby making, and more about his happiness. What he wanted for the future and how she could be more supportive of that.

"Are you going home today?" Gretchen asked.

"I'm not sure exactly when I'll be heading to the city." Even if he had planned on going home, he wasn't sure telling anyone other than his immediate family, and Tiki, was a good idea. He wasn't that he didn't trust Gretchen. It was about protecting everything he held dear.

"Oh really. Are you still in Lake George with Tiki?"

"I am."

"I've always loved the few pictures you've shown. I bet the sunrises are amazing."

He smiled. "I'm watching one right now."

"I'm jealous. Send me a picture. Please. Outside of the tabloids, which I'm ignoring. Blah, it's raining here."

He chuckled. He didn't see the harm in sharing a picture or two. "Sure. No problem. Now trust me. When you land in New York City, go home. Take a day or two. Even if I end up at the office today, there is nothing I'll need. If that changes, I'll call you, okay?"

"Maybe." She chuckled. "You know me. I like to be busy. Try not to make another headline."

"I'm trying not to. Hang on. Let me get that picture for you." He pulled up his camera, snapping the orange and pink sky glowing over the clear blue waters below. He stared at the screen for a long moment. It showed the mountains in the background. The lake rippled from a boat that had passed earlier. The houses across the bay illuminated from the impending sunrise. It was like a postcard. He resented that he had lingering doubts. Tag had dug into every rumor and while there had been some truth, there was nothing nefarious.

But still, no one trusted her and now he questioned her every motive.

He shouldn't.

She'd stuck with him through some trying times and she didn't have to.

He sent the picture to Gretchen. It couldn't hurt.

"Did you get it?"

"Oh, my God. That's beautiful. Is that still on the island? I didn't know there were houses up there."

For a brief second, he paused, wondering if he should answer. "I'm just trying to stay out of the media's grasp. Now did you need something?" he asked, doing his best to be vague. "Aren't you supposed to be flying back to New York today?"

"I'm at the airport waiting for the crew to finish flight checks and all that," Gretchen said. "However, I got a frantic email this morning from Bonnie. She accidentally deleted your editorial notes. Again. With everything that is going on, Brandi and your father have made it so I have to jump through hoops to access things."

Lake laughed. He'd seen that email and Bonnie

could be a piece of work. It was probably sitting in her deleted folder, which she had no idea existed. "Yeah. It's a bit of a shit show. I can forward you the notes to send to Bonnie. Is there anything else you need?" He'd do that through the company email so there was full transparency.

"I guess I can wait until I get to the office to log into the system. I just don't understand why my remote access has been taken away."

"Because someone hacked the system. For now, the only ones with that kind of control are me, Brandi, and my dad," Lake said. "My personal email was compromised as well. Besides, there isn't anything you need to be doing. Relax. Take a few days. Seriously."

"You've got to be joking. Some of your authors are worried that you're going to orphan them."

"How do you know that?" He had received a few emails from concerned writers panicking over nothing, but he understood they were reacting to half-truths the media had reported. Until Grant Publishing made a statement, either internally or to the public, he would have to put out each individual fire. But those came to his email.

"They contacted me."

He pinched the bridge of his nose. Any email

that came to her via a company addy, he would have gotten a copy.

Not a single author who was upset over the headlines contacted Gretchen. If they had called the office, they would have been transferred to his voicemail. She did have access to that, but she wouldn't have been able to delete any messages, not that she knew that. And he checked the messages daily. Most authors didn't call. Only agents.

Five of them tried reaching him.

Two called his cell.

But they were personal friends.

"Who? And how?"

"Called my cell and I talked everyone off the cliff. I'm being called to board," Gretchen said. "I'll talk to you soon."

"Travel safe." He ended the call.

The sound of a squeaky door opening caught his attention. He glanced over his shoulder and groaned.

Tiki appeared wearing nothing but his white T-shirt. Her nipples poked at the fabric.

"Your landlord would have to arrest you for indecent exposure." He set his phone on the railing and dropped his feet to the floor, making room on his lap.

The shirt lifted slightly when she sat, showing off the lack of panties.

"Commando?"

"I thought about coming out totally naked."

"So much for last night being—well—the last time." He cupped her breast, letting the weight of it fall into his palm. He leaned in and kissed her neck.

"Who were you talking to?" she asked.

"Gretchen," he whispered.

"Do we know when you have to return to the city?"

"Not in the next few hours." He moved his lips lower, tugging at the shirt, exposing her taut nipple. "I'm not in a hurry."

"I fear if you don't leave, we won't stop."

He lifted his gaze. "Would that be so bad?"

She dropped her forehead to his and sighed. "You're supposed to be a rebound. A fling. But I find myself caring about you and that's dangerous."

"I know." He palmed her face, running his thumb across her cheek. "We're in a crazy situation and eventually, I will be returning to New York and going back to my job." He closed his eyes and inhaled sharply. "When I was a little boy, my dad would take me camping and I would dream about having a place away from the city. Or even leaving the city altogether. It's so stifling there. But I've always had to live there because my family's there. And so is the family business."

"I find it interesting that you prioritize family over the publishing company."

"They go hand in hand," he admitted. "I love my parents, as flawed as they are. I don't agree with everything they are doing and honestly, my dad has always known the day he retires, is the day my sister and I start figuring out how I become a published author and she runs the business."

"You're an incredibly loyal son. You could have walked away and moved to a place that sang to your soul if you wanted to."

"But publishing is part of who I am. I want to figure out how to have both." He waved a hand toward the lake. "My family legacy and life like this."

"That's a tall order," she said. "But people work remotely all the time. It's become a thing."

He took her chin with his thumb and forefinger. "You and I, we don't date. We don't do relationships."

"You were the one who said that. I believe I just agreed I could get on board with it."

"What exactly are we discussing here?" he asked. "Because it feels like we could be talking about me spending a lot of time in this particular area of New

York State and us really getting to know one another." He pressed his finger over her lips. "Outside of the publishing world."

"It does sound like I might be suggesting that."

"I would hate myself if I ever hurt you." He lifted her into his arms as he stood, carrying her toward the door.

"I've taken the easy road most of my life because I was afraid of being hurt and look what happened."

He narrowed his stare. "Josh is an asshole who doesn't deserve a woman like you."

She smiled. "You're a sweet man. And you're right. But my point is I'd rather take a risk with something that is exciting and makes me feel good than something that doesn't even make my pulse increase. Life is filled with pain and the truth is, the only real agony I felt from Josh was self-inflicted."

Gently, he laid her on the bed and removed his clothing. His heart ached to follow his dream. To throw caution to the wind and do the unexpected.

But he knew he couldn't run away.

He had responsibilities to his authors.

To his mother.

His sister.

And to his father.

He stayed with the company because part of him belonged there and he couldn't walk away.

But now he needed to examine why he'd chosen not to allow himself to fall in love. Why he'd closed himself off from the prospect.

He came to one conclusion.

Everyone he'd ever met would have tied him permanently to the city. His parents introduced him to society women. Ladies who had deep connections to the world in which he'd grown up.

The women he dated were outliers, not because they weren't from New York City, but because they weren't the settling down type. They didn't want families any more than Lake thought he did.

Tiki changed everything.

And he had no idea how that had happened. He had no desire to fight it either.

"I don't know the first thing about being in a real committed relationship." He took her naked into his arms, kissing her cheek, neck, and center of her chest, making his way across her soft stomach. "I can't promise you I will be a good boyfriend, but I want to try."

She cupped his face, tilting his head. "Did you just use the *B* word?"

"Scary, right?"

"Terrifying that I'm not jumping out of this bed."

He went back to giving her body all the attention. His mind filled with different ways he could show her how much he cared. His heart swelled with new emotions he had no idea how to sort, but he enjoyed the way they scorched his skin. "It will have to be long distance at first. Weekends and when I can get away while my family and I figure out—"

"Stop talking." She curled his fingers around his length.

He moaned. "Yes, ma'am."

A soft breeze flowed through the open window. It smelled like sunshine and mountains.

He couldn't get enough of Tiki. Making love to her was like floating into a dream where he didn't ever want to wake up. She was the sweetest, kindest woman he'd ever known. She was absolutely too good for him and he could only hope that over time he'd learn how to be the kind of man she deserved.

Her climax rolled across her body and into his like a tidal wave. It grabbed ahold of his, pulling it out of his body in one swift motion.

He shuddered. It took a good five minutes before he could take a regular breath.

Propping himself up with a couple of pillows, he

tucked her into his side, running his hand up and down her arm. "Tell me something."

She glanced up. "What?"

"If you could live anywhere, money not being an object, where would it be?"

"Money is always part of the equation, even if you have it." She arched a brow. "So, when I think about that, I like to be realistic."

"All right. So tell me where and what that entails."

She scooted to a sitting position. "Do you see that house on the end of the point there?"

"Yes."

"That's Katie and Jacob Donovan's place."

"The private investigator?"

"That's the one," Tiki said. "Across from that is Cleverdale Point. You see that big white house?"

He nodded.

"That's where Jared lives. I live right behind it in his carriage house."

"Wow. That's nice. It's a little bigger than I had pictured."

"I like it there. But down the road and on the other side, so facing the other bay, is where my family lives. Right next door is where Gael and Tayla live. I wouldn't mind owning a place someday between where Katie's house is and Jared's place. That's still way out of my price range right now, but someday it could be doable."

His mind exploded. It was too soon to be buying places together, but if he was going to have a relationship with Tiki, he was going to need a place he could call his own. Not to mention, if he did end up having a book career, a place to write.

He knew he was months away from this entire idea; however, his mother always reminded him that dreams did come true.

A knock at the door snapped him back to reality.

"Are you two awake?" Foster asked. "I'm getting ready to make breakfast if you're hungry."

"We'll be there in ten minutes," Lake said.

"Coffee will be ready."

"Guess we better put our clothes back on," Lake said. "And I need to go back outside and get my phone. My dad is expecting to hear from me by nine."

"What do you think changed his mind about you writing and your sister being more of the head of the company?"

"Honestly?" Lake eased from the bed and found his clothing. "You."

14

"What the hell is going on?" Tiki swallowed. Hard. There were boats floating out front and vans parked across the street.

"Obviously, they found you." Foster tapped away on his cell. "Jared is sending over one of his troopers and a Lake George Patrol is two minutes away. Also, your dad is pulling in."

"Seriously?" Tiki let out a slow breath. "The last person I want to deal with is my dad."

"Tonya's coming with him. We're still going to collect your things."

"I guess I should be glad he left my mother at home," Tiki said.

"Relax." Lake stood behind her and rubbed her

shoulders. "I'll call my dad about doing a press conference right here. It will put an end to all of this."

Foster opened the front door. "Hello, Mr. Johnson."

"Foster," her father said. "It's good to see you, but sorry to be invading your space."

"No worries." He gave Tonya a hug and kissed her cheek. "I'm always happy to help out. Lord knows you and your family have always been there for me."

"Hi, Daddy." Tiki embraced her father.

"How are you holding up?" her father asked.

"I've been better," she said. "I'd like you to meet Lake Grant."

"It's nice to meet you, sir." Lake stretched out his hand. "Though, I wish it were under better circumstances."

"Me too." Her father glanced around the room with a crinkled brow. "Have any of you seen the news this morning?"

"My internet is down," Foster said. "I was headed outside to look at the connection when I noticed all the reporters. Ten minutes later, you called."

"What on earth have you three been doing all morning?" her father asked. "Playing Parcheesi?"

"We had breakfast and we've been—"

Her father interrupted her. "It was a rhetorical question." He held out his hand. "Give me your cell."

She did as requested. Her father tapped aggressively on the screen and then handed it back.

"Your mother and I got a phone call about the pictures and they made all the morning news shows," her father said.

"How the hell did they know where we were so fast?" Tiki stared at the picture of her half-naked body sitting on Lake's lap. She shook her head in disgust and swiped to another article on her phone. A dozen news outlets had picked up the story and were circulating the same five images.

All taken during their hot and heavy make-out session less than two hours ago.

Lake stood over her shoulder. "What the... That isn't true," he said. He pointed to the screen. "Please tell me that's a bald-faced lie."

"It is." Tears welled in her eyes as she read the paragraph about her breakup with Josh. How it painted her out to be the other woman. "But Jules could be pregnant. I don't know."

"Even if she is, he's the one who cheated on you," her father said. "He's the jerk."

She continued to scan another article. Her heart

dropped to her heels. "Oh no," she said. "Daddy, they are saying that I tried to be a writer and failed. That there is proof that I've already been rejected by Grant Publishing."

"Put it away," Tonya said.

"Yeah. You've seen enough." Her father put a firm arm around her shoulder. "You know that's not true."

"And so do I and I'll be able to prove it. We keep records of that stuff." Lake took her hand and squeezed. "Its obvious someone is feeding the press all this bogus information."

"How do we find out who and make them go away?" she asked.

"I'm not sure how to do the latter just yet." Lake stood by the picture window with his arms folded across his chest. He kept his gaze on the mountains. Or maybe it was Cleverdale or Rockefeller Point. "But I think I know how they found us."

"How?" she asked.

"I need to call my father." Lake pulled out his cell. "I'll be right back."

"Where are you going?" she asked.

"The boathouse. I know they will be watching me walk from here to there, and maybe even take a picture or two. But there is no story in that. Or none that I care about. I'll be right back." He didn't even glance over his shoulder as he headed for the door.

Tiki plopped down onto the sofa.

Her father sat on one side and Tonya on the other, both wrapping a protective arm around her.

"You really care about this young man, don't you?" her father said.

"I do. I don't know why or how it happened so fast, but he matters to me, and I'll walk away from writing if that's what it takes to save his reputation."

∽

LAKE TOOK the stairs toward the waterfront two at a time.

"Lake. Why all the mystery around the lady in your life? Is it because of her sordid past? The fact that you already rejected her? Do your parents not approve?"

He ignored the insanity and raced into the room he shared with Tiki last night. "Hey Siri, call Dad."

It rang twice.

"I was just about to call you," his father said.

"I fucked up, Dad. Big-time."

"If you're talking about Gretchen, stop. You couldn't have known."

"How do you know this is about Gretchen?" He pinched the bridge of his nose and decided to keep talking. "I sent her a picture this morning of the sunrise. That's how they found me. But what the hell is up with the rest of this bullshit? These stories are bogus."

"I just got off the phone with Tag and that PI whom Tiki's family knows, Katie Donovan. She's good. Really good. Tag is seriously impressed."

"What did they find out? Because Gretchen is going to be landing in New York soon."

"Son, she never left," his father said. "She sent a look-alike on our plane to the Bahamas. She's actually in Lake George. Katie's partner, Jackson, has eyes on her. She's been staying at the Motor Lodge in the village."

"My God. That's right across the road from where I rented the boat. She must have followed me." Lake sat on the edge of the bed. "She's one patient woman to have waited this long for me to do something that would give her ammunition to destroy me. Destroy the business."

"Don't be so hard on yourself and she's not going to get away with it," his father said. "Tag, with the help of Katie's people, has been able to find the planted manuscript that you supposedly rejected.

Katie's husband is a former FBI agent, so he's got a lot of contacts and they've discovered how she's been able to use back doors into our system to alter emails and all sorts of shit."

"So, what's the plan?"

"We're going to beat her at her own game," his father said. "But first, we need to give them another hour or two. And then you and Tiki will go in front of the press. And I guess a good place to do it will be right under her nose."

"Remind me not to piss you off."

His father laughed, then cleared his throat. "All of this is my fault."

"How can you say that? I'm the one who insisted we keep Gretchen after the Kacey incident."

"Because if I had listened to you and Brandi, there wouldn't have been a Kacey incident to begin with."

"The only good thing that's going to come out of this is Tiki. She's amazing. Not just the writing. She's—I don't know how to describe it all."

"What are you saying?" his father asked.

"It's way too early to say Mom might get her wish, but I think I might be falling in love."

15

Lake slowed the boat and took Tiki's hand. "Are you ready for this?" The rental docks were only twenty-five feet away. He could already see a crowd gathering in the parking lot across from the Motor Lodge.

"I'm ready for this to be over. So, yes."

Lake admired her resolve considering Gretchen had leaked the fake manuscript. Well, it wasn't completely fake. She'd taken the partial that Tiki had sent to Lake's personal Gmail account. Then she added a standard rejection letter with Tiki's name on it.

There were no timestamped emails in the server, so Lake did have some recourse. However, had they not had other proof of Gretchen's debauchery, it wouldn't have been enough.

But they managed to get the security footage from the private airport hangar that proved Gretchen never got on that plane. They also had pictures of the girl in the Bahamas, thanks to her social media account. Not to mention her willingness to roll over when the cops got involved.

Lake could easily let the police handle it all. However, Gretchen didn't just mess with him; she also fucked with Tiki, and even if he wasn't falling head over heels for her, he'd still want to go after Gretchen in the press.

His company would survive.

His reputation would repair itself over time.

It wasn't the end of the world for him or anyone in his family. They'd been dealing with scandal for decades and they always managed to come out on top.

But for Tiki, it could destroy a promising career before it started.

"Your friend Jared will be able to hear everything, and according to Tag and Katie, Gretchen is in that hotel across the street. The hotel manager said she hasn't left since she got her breakfast and the morning paper."

"What if I say the wrong thing?"

"That's impossible." He leaned in and kissed her cheek. "Just tell the truth."

"I can't believe Jared is going along with this. I mean, it's a spectacle and he hates those." She moved toward the stern, ready with the rope.

"Maybe, but he didn't like the pictures and he wants her to be as humiliated as we were. He said something about you deserving a break and if he could pull Josh over for speeding and it not be considered harassment, he'd do it. So this is the next best thing."

"You've got to love Jared."

"I really hope you mean that in a brotherly fashion."

"Are you jealous?" She tossed the line to the attendant.

The sound of cameras clicking in the distance grated on his every nerve. He did his best to keep those emotions in check for Tiki's sake, but part of him wanted to haul off and hit someone.

"What if I am?" He shut the engine down and pulled a ten from his pocket, handing it to the attendant, who shook his head.

"Thanks, but I'm sorry, sir. I work security for the

Heritage Inn," the young man said. "Which is owned by an ex-state trooper. I'm here to make sure all this goes down as planned. I can't take your money."

"I appreciate that," Lake said. "But that makes me want to give you more." He pulled out a twenty and stuffed it in the security guard's shirt. "Besides, it will look legit with all these reporters, and while you're standing here, answer me this. What makes this Jared guy so special? Even my girl here is practically drooling over him. I've met him. He's not that good-looking."

"You're joking, right? If there was a state trooper centerfold, he'd be it." The young man laughed. "But half of what makes Mr. Blake so appealing is his wife. However, I'm partial to his daughter, Chelsea."

"Aren't you a little old for her?" Tiki asked.

"I'm only nineteen and she's seventeen." The young man puffed out his chest. "But Mr. Blake's not too keen on the idea of me taking her out on a date. Even Mrs. Blake says he still lives in the dark ages. She says I have to find ways to keep on his good side. So, I work for his buddy while I finish my two-year degree in criminal justice before going to the State Police Academy."

"That's impressive," Lake said.

"Thank you, sir. I hope Mr. Blake thinks so too. I really care about Chelsea." The boy finished tying up the boat.

"What's your name?" Lake asked.

"Calvin."

"I'll be sure to tell Jared what a great job you did here," Lake said.

"Thank you. But my job is not done. Now I have to keep an eye out for this woman." He held up his phone. "I'm to perch myself on this dock because I've got a great view of the hotel room she's staying in. Once she steps foot outside, if she does, I'm to text Mr. Blake right away."

"Add me to that text." Lake handed him his card and another twenty. "And then I might have you do one more thing. With Jared's permission, of course."

But Calvin pushed the money back. "I'm sorry. But I really can't take any more. I appreciate it, but I'm not here for any monetary payout. I truly want to be a police officer and serving my community is important."

"I'm personally going to tell Jared he's nuts for not letting you date his daughter." Lake slapped Calvin on the back before taking Tiki by the elbow and guiding her down the dock. "He seems like a nice boy."

"He does," she said with a little laughter in her voice. "He's also, like most teenagers, slightly terrified of Jared. I do feel a little bad for his kids. Especially his daughter. She's gorgeous and gives her father a run for his money, but she's a good kid."

"Well, when I have kids—"

Tiki stopped dead in her tracks. "Excuse me?"

"If I have kids?" He scrunched his face. "I'm starting to change my mind on a lot of things since I met you."

"That's not a conversation I'm ready to have," she said. "We need to get through this scandal, and then maybe we might talk about how often I want you to come visit, but full-on future, we're not ready for that."

"What about the *L* word? Where do we stand on that?"

"Do you want me to push you in the lake? Because I will," she said.

He laughed. "Okay. Deal with saving your reputation and then declaring my undying love for you."

"You're crazy."

"In love." He winked.

"I'm not saying it back."

"I can wait," he said. "But only a few days. Then my ego might get hurt." He gave her a little hip check. "I'm kidding. Well, not about my feelings, but about the pressure. We have all the time in the world after we deal with this."

~

Tiki had never been at a press conference, much less given one before. She stood next to Lake behind the podium and glanced around the parking lot. Both her sisters had come. Gael and Foster were there. Her mom and dad. Her grandfather. Half the neighborhood.

Thankfully, Josh and Jules had opted to stay home.

A bunch of state troopers whom she'd met through Jared were either in uniform, officially working, or there helping out.

Lake placed his cell on the podium and covered the microphone. He leaned close. "My father and sister are in that big fancy dark SUV in the back of the parking lot," he whispered.

"How'd they get here so fast?"

"Private jet," he said. "But I'm glad. I look forward to you meeting them. I just wish my mom was here, but she's standing by at a studio in New York City to do an interview right after this so the focus can be brought back on her, which is how it should be."

"Can we get this over with?"

"Let's do it." He removed his hand, although the mic hadn't been turned on. He flipped the switch and tapped it. It made a loud noise. "I want to thank everyone for coming."

Lights flashed. Camera shutters clicked.

People inched closer.

A few of them shouted their questions.

Lake raised his hand. "Before we answer anything, I have a statement to read." He took out a piece of paper and unfolded it. "A couple of years ago, my family's publishing company had picked up Kacey Bromely after she'd been dropped by a competitor. We published three novels that hit the *USA Today* list, though they didn't stay on the list very long. We were in talks with her for a new series when she and I entered into an agreement for a possible collaboration."

Shouts erupted from the crowd.

"If you don't let me make the statement, I won't answer your questions," Lake said.

Every reporter backed down.

"Later I learned Kacey didn't want to have a writing partnership and when I denied her advances, she accused me of sexual harassment. That has been proven false and I will not speak of that. However, someone who was close to her at the time ended up coming to work for me. I thought this person had been duped as I had. I was sorely mistaken. For the past three years, Gretchen Colby, my assistant, has been waiting patiently to destroy my good name, along with my entire family, all because I not only didn't want to marry Kacey, but when we decided to no longer publish her, Kacey blamed us for her failing career." Lake held up his hand when more reporters shouted questions. "Kacey was no longer under contact with Grant Publishing. My agreement with her was never executed. We had no control over what happened to her career after the lies that she told."

Tiki was more than impressed by the way Lake handled himself. If it had been her to give the speech, she would have crumbled into a lump of tears by now.

"What many of you have reported recently—both online and in print—can be considered slanderous. You were given falsified documentation."

"Like what?" a reporter shouted. "And can you prove it?"

"The biggest lies are about my girlfriend, Tiki

Johnson. We will be making an official written statement regarding the facts. However, you have just about everything wrong. Tiki did not submit a manuscript to me a year ago, and yes, I can prove it. She is, however, in negotiations with us for a book deal. I can't and won't get into the details of that contract until it's been hammered out. But everything you've been given was either a complete fabrication by Gretchen or she stole it and our IT team has been working with the FBI and local authorities. This morning they were able to get the necessary proof to make an arrest for corporate sabotage and slander, among other things."

Lake's phone buzzed.

She glanced down and quickly read the text that indicated that Gretchen had stepped from her hotel room.

They couldn't see her from their location behind the podium, but the reporters could from the parking lot.

Game on.

Hopefully, Jared wouldn't be too mad at Calvin. This wasn't his idea.

"Why would Gretchen do this?" another reporter asked.

Tiki took the cell and as discreetly as possible,

she texted a message to Jared and Calvin, telling Calvin it was time to call attention to Gretchen. That hadn't been the plan. The authorities wanted to quietly take her in after allowing Lake and his family to make a statement. Jared thought that would be enough.

Lake wanted her to have a taste of what it felt like to be the center of negative attention. Granted, the story would turn anyway, and she'd be the topic of the conversation.

Not Tiki or Lake.

But Tiki had to admit, she wanted to see what Gretchen would do when the reporters stormed her with their microphones and their questions.

Jared immediately responded with a thumbs-up.

Nice.

Tiki set the phone down.

Lake placed his hand on the small of her back, drawing her closer. "We believe it has to do with revenge for her friend Kacey."

"Hey. Look." Calvin appeared from the other side of the podium, lunging into the crowd and pointing toward the motel across the parking lot. "Isn't that Gretchen over there, talking with the police?"

Every single person standing there turned their

head and there was a collective gasp right before the crowd rushed toward Gretchen.

Tiki needed to see Gretchen. To see her face. Her expression. To make contact with the woman who turned her world upside down when she was exposed for the fraud that she was. How dare she mess with Tiki's reputation.

Or Lake's and his family's.

She stepped around the podium.

"What are you doing?" Lake tugged at her hand.

"I need to watch this." She shrugged free, dashing into the crowd. She raised up on tiptoe.

Lake rushed to her side, wrapping his arm around her waist. "Stay behind the crowd. This could get ugly."

God, she hoped so.

Jared's men held the reporters at a safe distance while he and an FBI agent showed their badges and spoke to Gretchen.

"Gretchen, is it true? Did you try to sabotage your boss? Are you the one who called in all these anonymous tips to the press?" one reporter asked.

"Why'd you do it, Gretchen? What has Tiki Johnson ever done to you?" another one asked.

Gretchen stood there, wearing a big hat and

trying to shield her face by holding up her hand. She shook her head and said nothing.

The FBI agent asked her name and began citing her rights.

"This is bullshit," Gretchen said. "I'm being set up." She pointed her finger. "He's once again using his power and money to shut people up. Just like he did with Kacey. Her career is crap, thanks to him. She can't get a decent book deal because he destroyed her reputation. All I did was bring to light how he manipulates people. Especially women. The things he's had me do. The writers he's rejected because they wouldn't accept his advances. The only reason she's getting a deal is because she's sleeping with him and I have proof."

"No, you don't," Lake said.

"Just remember, everything you say can be used against you," Jared said. "I recommend getting a lawyer because I've seen the evidence against you and it's pretty damning."

"I'm sure it's all circumstantial," Gretchen said.

"No, it's not," a female voice boomed across the air.

Tiki turned and gasped. "What is Kacey Bromely doing here?"

Lake couldn't believe his eyes. He blinked at least a dozen times but that didn't change the fact that Kacey strolled across the pavement with his father on one side and their lawyer on the other.

The reporters had gone wild. Lake couldn't make out a single thing anyone was saying. Jared had a bullhorn and was doing his best to control things.

It took a good five minutes for the crowd to settle.

One of the reporters handed Kacey a microphone.

She cleared her throat, glancing in Lake's direction, making eye contact.

He sucked in a deep breath. "This is an unexpected turn of events."

"You can say that again," Tiki said.

"I'd like to clear up a few things," Kacey said. "However, before I do that, I'd like to apologize to Lake and his girlfriend, Tiki Johnson, for my part in this entire mess. I never intended for it to go this far."

"Don't listen to her," Gretchen yelled. "Lake and his family have paid her off."

Lake took Tiki's hand. "This should be interesting."

"Life is stranger than fiction," she whispered.

There was no truer statement.

"Actually, the Grant family hasn't given me a thing. When the story broke this morning, I called Chandler Grant myself. I knew I couldn't be a part of destroying an innocent woman who did nothing wrong. And the reality is, neither did Lake. Not to me three years ago, and not now," Kacey said. "I have turned over all text messages and emails I've had with Gretchen regarding her plot to take down Lake. I take full ownership of having those conversations. I pleaded with Gretchen not to do it, but she wouldn't listen."

"If you're the one who felt wronged, why would Gretchen continue?" a reporter asked.

"Gretchen submitted work three times under different pen names and Lake rejected her," Kacey said. "I told her to go to other houses. She's not a bad writer, but she had her heart set on Grant Publishing. However, I have to wonder if it's more about Lake than getting her work seen."

"Shit," Lake whispered. "I can actually guess which ones they were based on how hard she pushed a few."

"That clears up a lot," Tiki said.

Lake turned, ignoring the crowd. They were

focused on interviewing Kacey and snapping pictures of Gretchen being tucked into the back of a police vehicle.

"While the worst of this is over, there will still be lingering questions and everyone is going to want to know our status," he said.

"That's a very dry way of describing our relationship."

"Is that what we have?" he asked, pulling her closer.

She wrapped her arms around his shoulders and smiled. "I expect you to come to me at least one weekend a month. I'll come to you the same. We'll see how we feel the other weekends."

"Nope. That doesn't work for me." He kissed her nose. "I will be up here as much as I can. I'm even thinking about buying a place."

"Don't go crazy." She pressed her finger over his lips. "And let me ease into that *L* word. I need time to adjust to all of this. Okay?"

His heart lifted. "I know we're going warp-speed and I get we need to slow down. And we will. I've never felt like this for anyone and I have to admit as exciting as it is, it's a bit scary too."

She palmed his cheek. "When I got in my parents' boat and drove to that island, I thought all my dreams had been shattered. I had no idea that they were just beginning."

Lake pressed his lips over hers in a soft, romantic kiss. He was well aware that the reporters clicked a few strategic photographs.

But this time, they'd be spreading a truth.

Lake Grant was—indeed—off the market.

16

TAYLA AND GAEL'S WEDDING...

Tiki took her sister's bouquet as she climbed aboard Foster's wedding boat for the ride around the bay.

This one was on the house.

Tayla glanced up and smiled. "I'm married," she said. "To this guy." Tears welled in her eyes.

"I'm the luckiest man in the world." Gael wrapped his arm around Tayla and kissed her temple. "We'll see you all in a few days." He waved.

Foster pushed down on the throttle.

Tonya rested her head on her sister's shoulder. "I never would have guessed she would be the first one of us to get married."

"Me neither."

"And you're next." Tonya tugged at the bouquet.

"Ha ha."

Exhaustion seeped into every muscle in Tiki's body. The last few weeks had been filled with interviews with the FBI, state police, and the NYPD. Not to mention a few select reporters.

Thankfully, Gretchen took the plea deal.

She faced real prison time, fines, and the shame that went with what she'd done.

Tiki was just glad it was over and she and her family could get back to their normal lives.

Though nothing would ever be the same again.

She took Tonya's hand and strolled up the dock toward the rest of the crowd.

She smiled as she listened to her mother and Lake's mom discuss movies and television. It was an interesting and comical discussion. Her mom was still suffering from being a fangirl, but she was getting better now that this was their second dinner together.

Lake, her father, and Chandler were sitting around the firepit going over the paperwork for the house Lake had purchased two days ago. It was on Mason Road, not far from the Mason Jug and only a couple of miles from her parents'. Lake was trying to talk her into moving in. He didn't like the idea of her paying rent when he had this big beautiful house that he wouldn't be able to move into full-time for another year.

Even then, he would still have to spend time in the Big Apple every other month until his father retired.

However, they had worked out that Brandi would take over most of the day-to-day, allowing Lake to pursue his writing career. His projects would have to be approved by Brandi, his father, and one other acquiring editor. Lake was fine with all of that as long as the co-authoring project was still on the table.

Thanks to the minimal fallout from the Gretchen scandal, it was.

And they had given Tiki a three-book contract.

A good one.

She was still shocked at the deal.

She paused midstep and turned to her sister. "He wants me to move into the house."

"It's much nicer than Jared's carriage house."

"This is happening too fast."

"So?" Tonya said. "You're in love with him and he loves you. I don't see what the problem is."

"We'd be all but living together."

"Again, I don't see the problem. And Dad loves him. Gael is almost jealous," Tonya said.

"Yeah. That was kind of fun to watch." Tiki laughed, but it was cut short when she caught Lake's gaze. He smiled and winked.

Her knees buckled. Throughout the entire ceremony she couldn't stop thinking about how much she loved Lake. It was so easy to love him. Natural. As if she were born to love him and no one else.

They fit together like pieces of a puzzle.

"You haven't said those three little words yet, have you?" Tonya cocked her head. "What are you afraid of?"

"Making this even more real than it already is."

"Time to rip the Band-Aid off," Tonya said. "Hey, Lake. Can you come over here for a second? Tiki needs to talk to you."

"What did you do that for?" Tiki asked behind a tight jaw. But Tonya raced off, leaving her standing there in her bridesmaid dress, holding her sister's bouquet, while Lake sauntered across the yard like a sexy model straight off the cover of a romance novel. She sucked in a deep breath and let it out slowly.

But that didn't calm her nerves at all.

"What's up?" Lake ran his hands up and down her arms.

"I need to tell you something." Her heart pounded so loudly she figured he could hear it.

"I'm all ears."

"I've been thinking about the house," she said with a tremble in her voice. "And I think I'd like to move in."

"Really? Because that would make me so happy." He took the flowers and set them on the ground, heaving her to his chest. "For the next year, I'll be able to come up on weekends and maybe stay one week a month, except for when we're on deadline, but we'll work that out when we get to it."

"I know I said I wanted time and to slow all this down, but watching my sister get married today made me question why I'm refusing to tell you how I really feel."

"Uh-oh. Are we talking about the *L* word?"

Playfully, she slapped his shoulder.

"Tiki. I love you and deep down, I know you love me back. I feel it. If you're not ready to say—"

"I'm ready," she whispered.

"I'm listening."

"I love you, Lake Grant. With all that I am."

He brushed his lips over hers in a tender kiss. Any fears she had dissipated. He was her North Star. Her rock. Her guiding light.

She hadn't been looking for love, but she was glad she opened the door wide enough to let it in when she'd thought her dreams had been shattered.

"I should warn you that our mothers have started planning our wedding," he whispered.

"I'm not ready to discuss that yet, but when it does happen, I think a justice of the peace and a boat ride in Foster's vessel is about our style."

He wrapped his arms around her waist and lifted her feet off the ground. "You read my mind. Now, how about we go find a private place and practice wedding nights."

"You have a one-track mind."

"Yeah. It's called loving you," he whispered.

Thank you for taking the time to read *Shattered Dreams*. If you haven't already picked up the first book in the series, *An Inconvenient Flame,* please do and don't forget about book three, *The Wedding Driver*, which is Tonya and Foster's story!

Grab a glass of vino, kick back, relax, and let the romance roll in...

Sign up for my Newsletter (https://dl.bookfunnel.com/

[82gm8b9k4y](82gm8b9k4y)) where I often give away free books before publication.

Join my private Facebook group (https://www.facebook.com/groups/191706547909047/) where I post exclusive excerpts and discuss all things murder and love!

ABOUT THE AUTHOR

Jen Talty is the *USA Today* Bestselling Author of Contemporary Romance, Romantic Suspense, and Paranormal Romance. In the fall of 2020, her short story was selected and featured in a 1001 Dark Nights Anthology.

Regardless of the genre, her goal is to take you on a ride that will leave you floating under the sun with warmth in your heart. She writes stories about broken heroes and heroines who aren't necessarily looking for romance, but in the end, they find the kind of love books are written about :).

She first started writing while carting her kids to one hockey rink after the other, averaging 170 games per year between 3 kids in 2 countries and 5 states. Her first book, IN TWO WEEKS was originally published in 2007. In 2010 she helped form a publishing company (Cool Gus Publishing) with *NY*

Times Bestselling Author Bob Mayer where she ran the technical side of the business through 2016.

Jen is currently enjoying the next phase of her life... the empty nester! She and her husband reside in Jupiter, Florida.

Grab a glass of vino, kick back, relax, and let the romance roll in...

Sign up for my Newsletter (https://dl.bookfunnel. com/82gm8b9k4y) where I often give away free books before publication.

Join my private Facebook group (https://www.facebook. com/groups/191706547909047/) where I post exclusive excerpts and discuss all things murder and love!

Never miss a new release. Follow me on Amazon:amazon.com/author/jentalty

And on Bookbub: bookbub.com/authors/jentalty

ALSO BY JEN TALTY

Brand new series: SAFE HARBOR!

MINE TO KEEP

MINE TO SAVE

MINE TO PROTECT

Check out LOVE IN THE ADIRONDACKS!

SHATTERED DREAMS

AN INCONVENIENT FLAME

THE WEDDING DRIVER

NY STATE TROOPER SERIES (also set in the Adirondacks!)

In Two Weeks

Dark Water

Deadly Secrets

Murder in Paradise Bay

To Protect His own

Deadly Seduction

When A Stranger Calls

His Deadly Past

The Corkscrew Killer

Brand New Novella for the First Responders series

A spin-off from the NY State Troopers series

PLAYING WITH FIRE

PRIVATE CONVERSATION

THE RIGHT GROOM

AFTER THE FIRE

CAUGHT IN THE FLAMES

CHASING THE FIRE

Legacy Series

Dark Legacy

Legacy of Lies

Secret Legacy

Colorado Brotherhood Protectors

Fighting For Esme

Defending Raven

Fay's Six

Yellowstone Brotherhood Protectors

Guarding Payton

Candlewood Falls
RIVERS EDGE
THE BURIED SECRET
ITS IN HIS KISS
LIPS OF AN ANGEL

It's all in the Whiskey
JOHNNIE WALKER
GEORGIA MOON
JACK DANIELS
JIM BEAM
WHISKEY SOUR
WHISKEY COBBLER
WHISKEY SMASH
IRISH WHISKEY

The Monroes
COLOR ME YOURS
COLOR ME SMART
COLOR ME FREE

COLOR ME LUCKY

COLOR ME ICE

COLOR ME HOME

Search and Rescue

PROTECTING AINSLEY

PROTECTING CLOVER

PROTECTING OLYMPIA

PROTECTING FREEDOM

PROTECTING PRINCESS

PROTECTING MARLOWE

DELTA FORCE-NEXT GENERATION

SHIELDING JOLENE

SHIELDING AALYIAH

SHIELDING LAINE

The Men of Thief Lake

REKINDLED

DESTINY'S DREAM

Federal Investigators

JANE DOE'S RETURN

THE BUTTERFLY MURDERS

THE AEGIS NETWORK

The Sarich Brother

THE LIGHTHOUSE

HER LAST HOPE

THE LAST FLIGHT

THE RETURN HOME

THE MATRIARCH

More Aegis Network

MAX & MILIAN

A CHRISTMAS MIRACLE

SPINNING WHEELS

HOLIDAY'S VACATION

Special Forces Operation Alpha

BURNING DESIRE

BURNING KISS

BURNING SKIES

BURNING LIES

BURNING HEART

BURNING BED

REMEMBER ME ALWAYS

The Brotherhood Protectors

Out of the Wild

ROUGH JUSTICE

ROUGH AROUND THE EDGES

ROUGH RIDE

ROUGH EDGE

ROUGH BEAUTY

The Brotherhood Protectors

The Saving Series

SAVING LOVE

SAVING MAGNOLIA

SAVING LEATHER

Hot Hunks

Cove's Blind Date Blows Up

My Everyday Hero – Ledger

Tempting Tavor

Malachi's Mystic Assignment

Needing Neor

Holiday Romances

A CHRISTMAS GETAWAY

ALASKAN CHRISTMAS WHISPERS

CHRISTMAS IN THE SAND

Heroes & Heroines on the Field

TAKING A RISK

TEE TIME

A New Dawn

THE BLIND DATE

SPRING FLING

SUMMERS GONE

WINTER WEDDING

THE AWAKENING

The Collective Order

THE LOST SISTER

THE LOST SOLDIER

THE LOST SOUL

THE LOST CONNECTION

THE NEW ORDER

www.ingramcontent.com/pod-product-compliance
Lightning Source LLC
Chambersburg PA
CBHW052155240725
30132CB00008B/253